I0764504

THEM AIN'T THE BREAKS

A play in 2 acts

By Gregory John Ferris

© 2022 Gregory John Ferris

606 Oak Branch Road

Louisville KY 40245

5027975595

greggjferris@yahoo.com

Copyright 2022 by Gregory John Ferris

All rights reserved

Published by Oak Branch Publishing

ISBN

979-8-218-10723-9

A special thanks to Anne Harlan

THEM AIN'T THE BREAKS by Gregory John Ferris

CHARACTERS

ACINE FINLEY	Successful mystery writer, tired of her current life. Married to Keith for many years.
IEL HUFFIN	Widow, oldest friend of successful mystery writer Annacine. Naysayer.
H FINLEY	Annacine's devoted husband. Involved in many civic committees and activities.
G ROGUE	Owner of a local garage and classic car restoration shop
ERLY FREDRICHS	Friend of, and alter ego to Annacine. Attracts men, but so far has not been able to keep one.
Y MUSE	Young police detective sergeant

JASON SILVER	Young police detective. Emily's partner in the poli department
CHUCK and GENE	Poker player buddies of Keith

SETTING

The living room of Keith and Annacine Finley.

TIME

July 2017

SCENES

ACT I

Scene 1	Living Room	Early evening
Scene 2	Living Room	The following morning
Scene 3	Living Room	That afternoon
Scene 4	Living Room	That afternoon
Scene 5	Living Room	That afternoon

ACT II

Scene 1	Living Room	Morning, a week later
Scene 2	Living Room	Later that day
Scene 3	Living Room	Late evening
Scene 4	Living Room	A week later
Scene 5	Living Room	Evening
Scene 6	The Crime Scene	The next evening
Scene 7	The Crime Scene	10 minutes later

ACT I

SCENE 1

(The living room of Annacine and Keith, late morning. Annacine seated on couch, Keith enters, carrying a large potted palm, which he looks to place, finally deciding on a spot in a corner of the room.)

KEITH

What do you think of it, honey?

ANNACINE

What is it?

KEITH

It's a potted plant, like those in one of your mysteries. You haven't bought one for the house before and that surprises me. With all the guns, and knives laying around, I suppose you didn't think we had room for it.

ANNACINE

We don't have room for a potted plant.

KEITH

And the spear gun in my golf bag. You should have warned me, Annacine.

ANNACINE

How do you find three hours for golf, with all your other activities? You belong to half the organizations in town.

KEITH

All thanks to you my dear. You can write two murders and an acquittal in the time it takes me to chase one errant ball with the aid of a motorized cart. That reminds me, I need to ask Gary the pro at the club if I should have taken a penalty stroke for having an extra club in my bag, although I can't conceive of a situation in which I would use a speargun on a golf course.

ANNACINE

I can. Is there an event in golf not covered by the rules? The game has too many rules to be fun.

KEITH

The potted plant looks perfect here. As if it had been born here. Don't you agree, hon?

ANNACINE

I hate potted plants. That is why we don't have one. I detest potted plants. You should know that Keith, after how long we have been married.

KEITH

Twenty-five years, in a few weeks. (*Approaches and kisses Annacine*)

You detest potted plants; now I know. I detest having a noose hanging from the shower, and I detest having bottles of poison next to the vitamins in my nightstand. It's all part of your wonderful ability to balance work and home. What was the purpose for the noose, by the way? I noticed that it disappeared.

ANNACINE

It was a plot idea that did not work in real life.

KEITH

Thank goodness. The sound of water dripping from the hemp was so annoying, and the rope was beginning to turn green. I half expected it to sprout leaves. A potted plant is prettier and doesn't hog the hat water. A rope with leaves; would that constitute a crime, I wonder. Nowadays, legal and illegal seem to have swapped clothes. Really, I could not say no to this beauty. It's an exquisite shade of green, unlike that horrid rope.

ANNACINE

I hate plants, and I hate green. Combined into a green plant, it is just too much. That's why I decided to remove the noose from the shower. Green simply doesn't work in our bath. I expected the hemp to rot faster than nylon, but it was still too slow. Some things just don't leave as quickly as you wish. Anyway, the color green does not match our living room, either.

KEITH

Not even as an accent?

ANNACINE

Where on earth did you find it? It's hideous.

KEITH

The board at the orphanage gave it to me as a token of their appreciation for our support. If the folks at the orphanage had given me a hanging plant, I would have had to refuse it. I can still hear that drip, drip, like some story from Poe. And the smell. Sometimes I worry about you Annacine.

ANNACINE

By our support, you mean your support.

KEITH

Let me show you some pictures of the children we are helping. (*Sits beside Annacine*)

ANNACINE

I'm sorry, Keith. I forget how many worthwhile activities you are involved in.

KEITH

I don't have talent like you Annacine, I need to do something else to contribute.

ANNACINE

But why so many boards Keith? If there was an organization that managed other boards, I suppose that your membership there would be mandatory.

KEITH

Such an organization does exist, and I declined their invitation.

ANNACINE

How much is enough? Oh, you declined? Good. I never see you.

KEITH

I am trimming my involvement in more than a few organizations. It's time for a change. But now...
(*Turns to leave*)

ANNACINE

Where are you off to next, Keith? Tennis, more golf with a spear gun? Planning for a gala? Perhaps all three. Where do you find the energy?

KEITH

I'm lucky. It must come from good clean living, and a lack of stress.

ANNACINE

It is more that lack of stress. I've noticed that you are so chipper lately. Is it some secret change of life that comes over men?

KEITH

It could be. But I'm wonderful at keeping secrets, and I'm talented at understanding you.

ANNACINE

From studying my books? That would bother me. It would be creepy. We have no need of translators between us.

KEITH

It is unnecessary to read your books when I can read the author directly. What is troubling you, honey?

ANNACINE

You tell me.

KEITH

You need a back rub.

ANNACINE

I wish that was all it took. Do you have time?

KEITH

Of course, I do.

ANNACINE

You are bustling here and there more than ever. (*Settles in for backrub*)

KEITH

Aha. Bustling. Whenever you tell me I'm bustling, that confirms that you aren't able to write. You see my bustling (*shakes bustle*) you perceive it as a distraction. I suppose it is in a way (*wiggles bustle again*). And it prevents you from writing. You flip cause and effect. In fact, it's the other way round, because you can't write, you notice my...

ANNACINE

Please stop with the bustle (*laughs*)

KEITH

You notice me when you have too much time to kill, yet have no victims nearby and handy, ready to be obliterated. Since you don't consider murdering me polite behavior for a well-known mystery writer, you stab me with petty criticisms.

ANNACINE

Am I that obvious?

KEITH

To me you are. I doubt that many of your readers share a bed with a murderess. That has been part of your charm, along with your ability to knock off your characters in their sleep.

ANNACINE

That isn't difficult.

KEITH

But you murder them during your own slumber. You slay without pity. Do you stumble across them in a sort of shared literary dreamscape where the faster gun wins?

ANNACINE

My gun is empty.

KEITH

What?

ANNACINE

A little lower, oh, up just a bit Keith. Perfect.

KEITH

Relax Annacine, let my fingers knead away the stress, heating your skin where your worry can seep through the pores and evaporate like sweet perspiration in a tropical breeze.

ANNACINE

That sounds romantic.

KEITH

It is romantic. Open yourself to the quietly anticipated arrival of murder and mayhem.

ANNACINE

That line, not so romantic.

KEITH

(*Rubs Annacine's temples*). Anything? Any unpleasant thoughts?

ANNACINE

No, not yet. Oh, maybe...no. I've been there before; killed him. He was a nice guy; those make the best victims. Wait. Oh, no. Him too. Dead just the same but not nearly as nice a man. I rubbed him out quickly. As for you, keep rubbing. Perhaps violence will arrive naturally.

Rachel called earlier to say that she was stopping by.

KEITH

Rachel is insufferable.

ANNACINE

She is fine.

KEITH

In very small doses. I wish that she would stop stopping by.

ANNACINE

Rachel is invaluable.

KEITH

So is a trip to the dentist, but twice a year is sufficient.

ANNACINE

Rachel has her own calendar. She runs a day or a week or year behind me. I feel that I'm talking to my yesterday self. Regardless of what I suggest, her response is always the same. She tells me to stick to my knitting. And if I were tired of knitting, to retire. In her eyes I am a one trick pony.

KEITH

She sees me as an uncontrolled stallion in search of mares.

ANNACINE

Does that bother you?

KEITH

It bothers me. What would you do in retirement?

ANNACINE

Join boards like you. Or sit and the watch the clouds go by. But that would leave me idle at night unless I were to study the stars. Is it any wonder the Greeks invented gods. My god, they had nothing else to do.

KEITH

They should have created and joined a few boards.

ANNACINE

And when Rachel tells me something, there is a high probability that I should do the opposite.

KEITH

What does Kimberly say when you propose a new idea?

ANNACINE

If she ever agrees with Rachel, I will find myself in desperate need of a third soothsayer.

KEITH

A few may remain in Greece. We should go.

ANNACINE

This is Rachel:
I bring you news from the outside world. A tale of woe and intrigue that may lead to murder most foul.

KEITH

Does she really talk like that when you two are alone?

ANNACINE

No, but it renders her stories more interesting in the retelling.

KEITH

Rachel is a gossip.

ANNACINE

'A weaver of tales' lessens the insult, but yes, Rachel is a gossip

(*Doorbell rings*)

KEITH/ANNACINE

Damn!

ANNACINE

It's not your fault, Keith. I've a headache. I simply can't assassinate tonight, honey.

(*Keith answers door, while Annacine remains prostrate.* RACHEL *enters quickly*)

KEITH

Hello, Rachel. More bustling has arrived honey, bearing the feminine touch.

RACHEL

Why are you lying about Annacine? Today is a beautiful summer day. You must be outside on such a fine evening, and not prostate here with some headache caused by "writer's block."

KEITH

How did you know?

RACHEL

Your dear wife missed our weekly coffee at Starbucks. What else could it be? She has little in life but her imaginary friends to keep her company, and when they stand her up, or she has sent them all to their graves, she regifts their dead absence by insulting her flesh and blood friends. I'm right, aren't I? Writer's block headache?

ANNACINE

It moved lower the moment you arrived.

RACHEL

Very funny. You should try writing comedy.

ANNACINE

You suggested that thirty years ago.

RACHEL

You ignored me at the time.

KEITH

Annacine has been miserable ever since. How many books is it now, honey? Sixty-two?

RACHEL

Isn't there somewhere that you need to be Keith?

KEITH

Other than in my own home, with my beautiful, successful wife? You tell me, Rachel.

RACHEL

Your husband is the most frenetic man I know, Annacine. You should engage an assistant to keep his itinerary.

KEITH

I have this (*little red book*).

RACHEL

How quaint. I have a similar one myself.

KEITH

A blind squirrel. For once, you are correct, Rachel. Annacine, I do have a meeting. Will you be ok for a few hours? (*Annacine nods*)

Are you sure?

ANNACINE

Yes, I will be fine.

RACHEL

What sort of meeting do you have at this hour?

KEITH

I am recording another Audible book at the Printing House for the Blind. It isn't one of Annacine's. (*Keith exits*)

RACHEL

You should steal a glance into his little black book. I don't' trust men with little black books.

ANNACINE

The little black book is red.

RACHEL

Don't be literal.

ANNACINE

My publisher and accountant have little imagination. They can't envision how I make them money with my books. In turn, they encourage me to be take things I say literally. I murder strangers for royalties. Accuracy and precision are demanded by my faithful readers.

RACHEL

Can you say the same thing about the man who just left?

ANNACINE

Keith? Why yes. His charitable activities are serious affairs that require accuracy and precision as much as my novels. On top of that he has the charm and perseverance that I lack.

RACHEL

You left out faithfulness.

ANNACINE

That goes without saying.

RACHEL

Does it?

ANNACINE

Faithfulness is read between the lines. I write mysteries, Rachel. I don't enjoy them in my personal life. But go on, who is Keith supposed to be seeing now? Tell me a story.

RACHEL

Why would you ask me such a thing?

ANNACINE

When I ask a woman to tell me a story, she invariably recounts her entire autobiography whereas with men is rarely about them. I find the latter much more interesting, and briefer. You are an exception.

RACHEL

Thank you.

ANNACINE

Rachel, you're my oldest friend.

RACHEL

I hope not as old friends die first. I may qualify as your longest-term friend

ANNACINE

And that hasn't aged you as it has me?

RACHEL

Why would it? There's something different about you today. I noticed it the other day as well. What is wrong? You can confide in me, your dearest friend. Unhappiness is like murder; its either booze, men, or money.

ANNACINE

Everyone I touch turns into a writer.

RACHEL

You don't drink much and you're rich, so it must be Keith.

ANNACINE

If I were a destitute lush, you would continue to target Keith.

RACHEL

Take those two and ditch Keith.

ANNACINE

Who is she?

RACHEL

In fact, Keith and I have a board meeting on the third Monday of every month, and if there is another woman involved, I've no doubt that her name is Faye Alexander.

ANNACINE

Such a friend you are, so quick with the name of a villain but, I'm afraid it won't work.

RACHEL

What does that mean, it won't work.

ANNACINE

I admit I don't fully understand mechanics of magic; in fact, I'm completely clueless when it comes to hocus pocus. I should research magic for my next murder, oh that's a problem, but it follows that if you christen a girl Faye, you consign her to insanity. So, you see it can't be this Faye Alexander. Her name is all wrong.

RACHEL

In one of your books, it may be but big surprise possibly to you there is more to the world in the books on the shelves. And you are wrong about the name Faye. Every Faye I've met has been someone you don't leave your husband alone with.

ANNACINE

Weren't you there with him at the board meeting? He wasn't alone then with a woman name Faye.

RACHEL

I suppose that you have a point. But he was sitting next to her.

ANNACINE

That's different. Let me know if he does it again next month.

RACHEL

We don't meet in August. I'll let you know after the September meeting. It is awfully suspicious, his attending charity events and raising funds for good causes. It isn't natural.

ANNACINE

I'm not natural, Rachel. I do murders and Keith does charity. He aids others and I eliminate them. It's a marriage made in Kentucky

RACHEL

Not in Heaven?

ANNACINE

It's almost identical except down here our horses don't have wings.

RACHEL

Well? What is the problem?

ANNACINE

My unhappiness. I want to change my writing. That is my blockage.

RACHEL

I generally agree that deciding to stop killing your fellow humans is the right decision, but in your case, given that your victims bleed only ink, I give you a pass. Slay on. You could try one of those new super pharmaceuticals they advertise late at night. Once you swallow one, if you aren't dead twenty minutes later you will be seeing if not riding winged horses, unable to pronounce the name of the super pharmaceutical. I'm sometimes tempted to try one myself, but...

ANNACINE

You are a dear friend. Only you can make me laugh the way you do.

RACHEL

Speaking of Keith, I saw him recently. Before today, that is.

ANNACINE

What did you speak about?

RACHEL

We didn't speak. He wasn't alone.

ANNACINE

Faye Alexander?

RACHEL

An anti-Faye Alexander. A genuine mystery woman.

ANNACINE

A real mystery woman? I would probably like her.

RACHEL

Have you ever killed your husband in one of your novels?

ANNACINE

They are not told in first person.

RACHEL

What?

ANNACINE

I'm not writing about myself.

RACHEL

I heard that the best novels were autobiographical. But yours, oh never mind. That would be unkind, and we are such good friends.

(*Annacine goes to bookshelf and touches a few of her works*)

ANNACINE

Sometimes I believe that I know you better than I know Keith. You are the town crier.

RACHEL

I've been called worse. Me, I prefer town watchman. Do you recall my late husband? He was constantly looking upwards and missed the world going by. He must have enjoyed it as he left explicit instructions that he be placed in the casket face up.

ANNACINE

That's normal Rachel.

RACHEL

Is it a normal request for a man who could not manage to sleep on his back? I can't tell you the number of times I would go to the toilet in the middle of the night and use his bare, shiny butt as a landmark. Of course, if had slept on his back, I'd have not found my way back until dawn's early light. He was not exactly mastful.

ANNACINE

How long has he been gone?

RACHEL

Long enough. Time flies when you are having fun. Speaking of husbands.

ANNACINE

Are you any closer to capturing another one?

RACHEL

Not me.

ANNACINE

Sorry. They are always in season.

RACHEL

You should stick with murder Annacine, as your humor is as much fun as a shotgun blast to the face. Speaking of husbands, it is regarding your husband I came to speak.

ANNACINE

Keith again?

RACHEL

He is still your husband.

ANNACINE

Of course, he is.

RACHEL

He hasn't given you two weeks' notice?

ANNACINE

I find your jokes as humorless as mine, but more repetitive. Who is it this time?

RACHEL

This time! Then it has happened before.

ANNACINE

No! And there is no this time, this time. All of your alarms have been false.

RACHEL

She's cute.

ANNACINE

And she is young, and slim and oozing whatever it is that cute, young, slim things are oozing in abundance this season.

RACHEL

You've seen her yourself?

ANNACINE

Only in print, from my book five to book fifty-three. She hasn't aged a wink; I will give her that. But then, I did grace her with the gift of eternal youth. Although she has come close to dying young a few times. You've spied this woman yourself, Rachel. Is her oozing still off the charts? I always worried about overdoing it, but I'm not certain of which scale measures ooze.

RACHEL

Wittiness is no substitute for keen eyesight Annacine. I've known you long enough to lie to you convincingly but too long to do so. Never mind I'll leave.

ANNACINE

I'm sorry. I've been under a lot of stress recently. Truth is so worthless that it invariably ends in the trashcan.

RACHEL

What is that thing?

ANNACINE

More trash. A potted plant.

RACHEL

You hate plants! Potted or otherwise unless you are using it to murder someone. There is an idea.

ANNACINE

Take it home with you; it's an orphan.

RACHEL

How would I transport it, Annacine? Look at it.

ANNACINE

I'm tired of looking at it. Take it home.

RACHEL

It's immense. Bulky and likely infested with insects.

ANNACINE

It should remind you of Stevie. Give the poor child a good home.

RACHEL

You don't like it?

ANNACINE

Truly, until this moment, I was ambivalent.

RACHEL

That's progress. And now?

ANNACINE

Now, I despise it. It's yours.

RACHEL

If I want it.

ANNACINE

Doubly so if you do not want it. It's pretty, in a green, clingy, flat sort of way. It resembles money without the bouquet.

RACHEL

Keep it yourself.

ANNACINE

It was a gift to Keith from some charity or another.

RACHEL

Keep it then. Charity stays at home, as they say. Or it should. As should husbands.

ANNACINE

He should have known that I can't abide plants in the home. Anyway, it clashes with the rest of the house.

RACHEL

How can one tiny, little insect covered, fetid houseplant clash with everything in this huge house? Spray it and be done with it.

ANNACINE

It clashes with me. Some folks refuse to have pets in their residences. I don't like plants.

RACHEL

I know that.

ANNACINE

As should Keith. Men can be as observant as a corn stalk. You've had plants before Rachel.

RACHEL

Stevie? (*Annacine nods*) Yes, dear Stevie was indoors for our entire marriage. And when he passed away, I took him to Cave Hill and had him planted there.

ANNACINE

Do you still miss him?

RACHEL

Oh sure. But not to the point of wishing for his return. I've not told anyone this, Annacine, but I was superstitious. Cave Hill is a beautiful cemetery. It's well kept, but eerie. I contacted the grave digger manager a few days before the service and paid him to excavate the grave two feet deeper than normal. I wanted to prevent any chance that Stevie would resprout.

ANNACINE

That explains the...plop is the word, I guess. I wondered what happened that day at the cemetery. I recall very distinctly the sound of a plop, or maybe thud is closer to the tone, as the burial detail realized that their straps were too short, and they collectively released their hold. It was the only time I've heard, "one, two, go" spoken over an open grave. It was like a final rock, paper, scissors. No two out of three.

RACHEL

The coffin flipped over as it dropped, so I link to think that he is sleeping the way he would find most comfortable. Anyway, Stevie went out with quite a thump. That's the only part of Stevie that I miss.

ANNACINE

The thump?

RACHEL

The thump.

ANNACINE

Rachel, take the plant as consolation. Call it Stevie.

RACHEL

Consolation? You don't understand the word very well for a writer. Can you have it delivered?

ANNACINE

I'm not Von Maur.

RACHEL

Move it to some corner until I can manage to take it.

ANNACINE

It is already in some corner. I'm in every corner with the darned thing.

RACHEL

I have a solution. Ask Keith to deliver it. He comes and goes here more than UPS.

ANNACINE

That won't work, Rachel. The plant is Keith's gift.

RACHEL

Men are so obstinate when it comes to regifting. My Stevie was an exception. He was an inveterate composter. Meeting him for the first time, you'd have thought that he had invented the concept.

ANNACINE

Well, he is still perfecting it, as we speak. I'm sorry, Rachel, that was cruel.

RACHEL

I wish I had thought of that line first. I'm going to use the joke myself if you haven't already copyrighted it.

ANNACINE

Have at it. Just so long as you take that plant away.

RACHEL

OK, you win. Give me a few days to make arrangements.

ANNACINE

Are you on her trail?

RACHEL

Am I on whose trail?

ANNACINE

The oozer.

RACHEL

It's none of my business I've better things to do than follow men and their floozies. You haven't replied to my question.

ANNACINE

Was there one?

RACHEL

Have you ever killed your husband?

ANNACINE

I did reply. The answer is no.

RACHEL

I don't care for that answer.

ANNACINE

Yes is better than no? Are you suggesting that I kill my husband?

RACHEL

Why not? You're good at murder and you haven't eliminated him yet.

ANNACINE

You did not kill Stevie by any chance did you?

RACHEL

He wasn't worth a preliminary hearing. He just faded away like a sunflower in winter.

ANNACINE

I've been thinking of giving up murder.

RACHEL

And do what in its place? You have one trick, like a..

ANNACINE

Write romance.

RACHEL

Finally a joke! You are so funny. I must dash. I will stop by later this week for the plant. Romance! You do have a sense of humor. (*Exits*)

ANNACINE

Rachel is always wrong, but she rarely makes a mistake.

ACT I

SCENE 2

(*Keith and Craig enter, both wiping their hands*)

KEITH

Let me take that Craig. Please, have a seat. My better half is at tennis and won't return for a while. (Exits to dispose of rags, returns in a minute with two beers. Craig examines bookshelves, awards, some sort of million seller gold record equivalent)

A toast to Annacine. Thanks to you Craig, she will be able to take the trip that is so long overdue.

CRAIG

I'll do my best. Parts can be hard to get, and costly.

KEITH

I understand. That is why I came to you , the best car restorer in the region.

CRAIG

I haven't worked on a DeSoto in a while, they are quite the ride for their time. I haven't seen anything amiss for a car show, but for an actual trip, it does need some maintenance. As long as the engine and transmission, work then we'll be fine. I will discover more down at the shop. There are fuel lines, exhaust, shocks, coolant, and that is the smaller items. The technology is old. A DeSoto is not a Tesla. It might get expensive quickly.

KEITH

And the brakes. Don't forget the brakes.

CRAIG

I won't. Them brakes are nothing to ignore. A 1955 DeSoto FireDome. It is a beauty. Have you considered installing seat belts?)

KEITH

I really prefer to keep the car original. A modern car is safer, but we will stick to back roads. Where would I stop once I began to modernize it? A new motor and airbags, advanced suspension.

CRAIG

You have an incredible stockpile of parts, but labor is the expensive part in your case. Parts would be pass through. If you like, you could pay my labor in parts.

KEITH

That's intriguing. Do you have another client with a De Soto?

CRAIG

No, not yet. I've been looking for one myself. That's why I decided to take on your restoration. Heck, it is not even a restoration, but more like minor neglected maintenance.

KEITH

Neglected maintenance. That is it exactly.

CRAIG

You could do this yourself and save on labor entirely. Like I indicated, I have a lot of things on my plate now that...

KEITH

I have far too many projects and commitments

CRAIG

Committees?

KEITH

Those as well.

CRAIG

May I ask you a personal question, Keith?

KEITH

Of course. Those are easier to answer than automotive ones.

CRAIG

Are you undercover?

KEITH

I stand corrected, it may not be an easy question. Undercover? In what way?

CRAIG

These books, all written by a woman named Annacine. And we've just drank a toast, one can do that with beer, right?

KEITH

Drink a toast with beer? That qualifies

CRAIG

We've drank to your car, Annacine.

KEITH

We have?

CRAIG

Is Annacine your pen name, oh what is the word?

KEITH

I'm puzzled Craig. My car? The DeSoto?

CRAIG

Pseudonym. That is the word I was thinking of. It has a strange sound, like the name of a part that might be found on a 1955s DeSoto. Like an early version of a capacitor. That is why I recall the word.

KEITH

I wish that I could recall your question. What exactly are you asking me? I'm not acing what should be an easy category.

CRAIG

All these books, and trophies.

KEITH

And awards.

CRAIG

Do you write these books under the name of a woman named Annacine? I've heard that men write romance books, but they sell better if they are thought to have been a woman's creation.

KEITH

To answer your questions. Some of the trophies and awards are mine, mostly the smaller ones with the miniscule font are mine, in my name.

The others, all the books without question, are the sole work of my wife, Annacine.

CRAIG

And the car is named after her?

KEITH

The toast we had a moment ago? That is to my wife, she hasn't had time to drive it, or to accompany me on a long trip in it, for many years. Her work takes priority.

CRAIG

What do you do?

KEITH

You are very good with asking difficult questions Craig. Charitable events, sports, clubs, snatches of time with Annacine when she is not murdering someone.

CRAIG

What?

KEITH

The books around us contain not the romance of life and love but are full of the darkness and finality of murder induced death in its awful, if alliterative variety. At last count, sixty-two shades of stabbings, shootings, and other means of silencing others.

CRAIG

Your wife must enjoy it.

KEITH

I suppose that she does.

CRAIG

You aren't certain, Keith? I hate to pry, but this work may cost a small fortune, if I am wrong about the car.

KEITH

I have the money.

CRAIG

It's more than a question of money. I like what I do. Like your wife does. Yeah, I genuinely enjoy it. I may not have restored sixty-two classics, but it is nearly that number. In all of those, I've only had one client stop halfway through. The car was never completed. Although the client had a valid excuse, he died during the restoration, it bothered me that his family abandoned our project and sold the car as is to a stranger in California.

KEITH

Craig, it is important to me and to Annacine that our project, as you phrased it, be completed. It is more than a long-delayed plan, more than a gift. The car is a means to an end. By the way, if you meet Annacine, please mention nothing about the restoration.

CRAIG

May we toast again, now that I understand everything?

KEITH

Here are the keys. Thanks again for accepting this, our project.

CRAIG

The engine and transmission will be as good as new, if they aren't already. The car will be in tip top shape, safe for a second honeymoon.

KEITH

And the brakes. Don't forget the brakes.

CRAIG

I won't.

ACT I

SCENE 3

ANNACINE

How are you and your latest doing? I forget his name but he's a playwright

KIMBERLY

We broke up.

ANNACINE

That's too bad.

KIMBERLY

I figured that a switch from amateur athletes was needed. Steroids and one and done go hand in hand, if you know what I mean. I used to be a fan of ESPN. As of now, it is ESP NO for me. Still, the intellectual route was a dead end. I should have broken up earlier. He was all write and no play. I need more romance.

ANNACINE

You've had more than I could ever write.

KIMBERLY

It doesn't take much to scribble a few words together. Not you, Annacine. What I meant to say was that Felix wanted to do nothing other than write. I need more passion than an erect stylo can provide. I felt like a lonely piece of paper, laying around, but no one willing to doodle me.

ANNACINE

That's why I have decided to change. I've murdered the last man.

KIMBERLY

You've annihilated them all? I guess that it doesn't matter as men don't read your books.

ANNACINE

Yes, they do.

KIMBERLY

Not anymore. Still, you could have left a few alive for me. A few for breeding stock would be pleasant.

ANNACINE

You don't want children. Or has that changed?

KIMBERLY

We could put them in a man preserve. It would be good for them, catch and release.

The ones I attract are half dead anyway and here you've made them extinct. They were cute, in their own way.

ANNACINE

Let me be more precise, I've killed my last man.

KIMBERLY

Keith? But your husband is, or was, a member of the good guy tribe. To Keith, the last of the Mohicans. Or should it be the last De Soto?

ANNACINE

Really, Kimberly, you can be so exasperating.

KIMBERLY

My being exasperating is what you don't pay me for, but in a perfect world, you would. I keep your creative juices flowing. Maybe you could scratch one up for me, a nice man, not too nice of course, that would not do, as I've done nice men, and they, well, enough unsaid about nice men, but sculpt one for me, the way you can do, with your pen. Its so easy for you, Annacine. Yes, a not so nice man intimately familiar with all things juicy.

ANNACINE

You desire that I doodle a doodler for you.

KIMBERLY

I knew that you'd understand.

ANNACINE

Perhaps I can. Actually, I know that I can. And I am.

KIMBERLY

Have you been secretly reading Doctor Seuss again?

ANNACINE

Cheating spouses, worthless inheritors, grouchy grandpas, faithless brothers.

KIMBERLY

That is not the good doctor Seuss. Where is the cat in the hat and his madcap mayhem?

ANNACINE

Deadly doctors. The list goes on and on, ad infinitum. I'm hip deep in inky blood. I've terminated my terminations.

KIMBERLY

Can you please halt this monologue and refill my glass? No poison, please.

ANNACINE

I've given up on adulterated alkaloids as well. But not on tannins.

KIMBERLY

It is time to open a bottle of the good stuff. I was always hesitant before, fearing that you might have forgotten an experiment with exploding Bordeaux. But now that you are reformed, rehabilitated, paroled...

ANNACINE

Stop. I'll open a wonderful vintage from the basement.

KIMBERLY

Pick one that requires a corkscrew. You're fortunate enough to have wine cellar, filled with vintage men, I mean wine. Are you serious about the murders?

ANNACINE

Yes, I've whacked my last womanizer. It came to me in a dream.

KIMBERLY

Tell me. I love hearing the dreams of other people, they are without fail nonerotic, so unlike mine. Why do you even go to sleep? Unless people lie about their nocturnal musings. Tell me the truth; are you lying?

ANNACINE

I'm dreaming. I'm driving. I'm on a road.

KIMBERLY

Your dream is putting me to sleep.. If it does, don't wake me. There are plenty of men where I'm going, considering you've disposed of all those with warm flesh and hot blood.

ANNACINE

Don't interrupt. The road is narrow, filed with twists. Its nighttime. I can smell the wet leaves on the trees, the damp of the earth, the musk of ferns. And at the end of the road, its

KIMBERLY

What, the brakes fail? An abyss? A cliff?

ANNACINE

I asked you not to interrupt. It was my dream. And at the end...

KIMBERLY

A shirtless man carrying a frowning jack o lantern and a bottle of cognac?

ANNACINE

I saw none of that Kimberly. Strange. You have a dark side that I never noticed before. I saw a McDonald's parking lot. In the middle of nowhere, in a spot perfect for any imaginable adventure, I found only a happy meal and a nearby dumpster to dispose of the garbage.

KIMBERLY

Wow! That was certainly a vision worth the retelling. An unexpected offramp to oblivion might have been preferable. Can we have wine now, mommy?

ANNACINE

I'll be back in a minute. (*Annacine exits*)

(*Keith and Craig enter.*)

KEITH

Oh, Hi Kimberly. I thought that I heard Annacine's voice before we walked in.

KIMBERLY

You did. She is down in the cellar.

KEITH

Kimberly, this is Craig Rogue. He stopped by to pick up the key to the trunk. I'll fetch it.

KIMBERLY

Craig. I remember now. You are the car guy. Vroom vroom.

CRAIG

Yeah, that's me. Do you like cars?

KIMBERLY

Sure. I guess.

CRAIG

Come see me when you are old enough to drive. We can go for a spin.

KIMBERLY

It might make you dizzy. I like men and cars.

CRAIG

We have something in common. I like cars and women. I can handle dizzy.

KIMBERLY

Here, take my card. It has my cell number if you need to reach me.

CRAIG

Reach you for what? Do you have a car in one of my shops?

KIMBERLY

Do you do house calls for women without licenses?

CRAIG

As a practice, no.

KIMBERLY

It could be a matter of safety.

CRAIG

I've been known to make exceptions for safety. Do you need your brakes checked?

KIMBERLY

Often several times a day. They overheat

(*Keith returns*)

KEITH

Here it is. I hate to push you out the door, but..

CRAIG

I understand. We can talk later. It was nice to meet you, Kimberly. Maybe we can talk later too.

KIMBERLY

When I have my driver's license?

CRAIG

I'm in the book.

KIMBERLY

The book? One of Annacine's?

CRAIG

I'm in the phone book. Keith has my number as well.

(*Craig exits*)

KEITH

What is Annacine doing in the basement?

KIMBERLY

She went down to fetch a bottle of wine. She has quite the variety to select from.

KEITH

Vintage?

KIMBERLY

Of course. Its nothing but the best for Annacine. I'm a wonderful vintage as well. I need to be uncorked too. You have a corkscrew, don't you? I should have asked the car guy, they are always prepared with their tools.

KEITH

I'm sure that there is one around here.

KIMBERLY

You have so many friends and charitable activities. Can't you take pity on me and find me...

KEITH

A corkscrew? Here it is.

KIMBERLY

(*Takes it from him, while holding his hand between hers.*)

I mentioned to Annacine only moments ago that you are a member of the good guy tribe. Every tribe needs a black sheep. Otherwise, how could you tell good from bad? The whole of civilization would collapse, not to mention Annacine's book sales. A flock requires someone who wields a staff, I forget the saying, but you understand what I'm saying. Some strong man, someone from your tribe, that is all that I am asking, Keith.

KEITH

We've discussed this before Kimberly.

(*Annacine returns.*)

KIMBERLY

What took you so long? Keith and I were warming up the corkscrew. Its on the verge of melting.

ANNACINE

I see.

KIMBERLY

You know what we were talking about a few moments ago?

ANNACINE

That was between us. I'll share when I'm ready.

KEITH

Share what, dear?

ANNACINE

A new book. Maybe.

KEITH

That is wonderful news. Are you going to throttle anyone we know?

ANNACINE

I just might.

KIMBERLY

Book, smook, its all paper over the dam. I'm talking about you finding me a fresh man. Well, Keith has agreed to help in the search. Since he's taken, that is. He is taken, isn't he? If not...

I'm joking you two. But seriously, I see no collaboration between you pair of lovebirds in bringing me an eagle. Two birds in the bush is better than an empty nest.

KEITH

Hon, I'm off to the park's meeting. And Kimberly, don't forget you agreed to attend the Breakers meeting tomorrow afternoon at 2.

ANNACINE

But you've just arrived. Rachel was right.

(*Keith exits*)

Gone again.

KIMBERLY

You missed Craig Rogue.

ANNACINE

Who?

KIMBERLY

The car guy.

ANNACINE

He came to the house with Keith?

KIMBERLY

Yes, but he stayed only a few moments.

ANNACINE

Are you certain that it was not Keith in disguise? One actor coming and going so quickly that you mistake one for two.

KIMBERLY

I could tell the difference.

ANNACINE

Keith knows so many more people in this town than I do.

KIMBERLY

You need to get out more often. Take a drive. Meet some new friends. See the world, or at least Henry County.

ANNACINE

I see dead people.

KIMBERLY

That has already been done. Dead people can be a downer. You have to carry the conversation, they won't buy you a drink, and they can't dance worth a damn. I wonder if that explains a few of my exes.

ANNACINE

The majority of my acquaintances are characters.

KIMBERLY

So are Keith's. , the car guy included.

ANNACINE

True enough.

KIMBERLY

The car guy included. I wonder what Craig is like out of costume. I gave him one of my cards.

ANNACINE

Those cards of yours are so rare and collectible. Only half of the single men in town have one. You are such a flirt.

KIMBERLY

One man is not enough.

ANNACINE

One right man is enough.

KIMBERLY

One at a time. That Craig is a real hunk.

ANNACINE

He is real I suppose, even if I haven't seen him. All of Keith's characters are real. Its short, simple, Craig the car guy, Keith the bon vivant, you the..

KIMBERLY

Your characters are genuine as well. They are more complex than Craig the car guy I bet. Kimberly the, I'm glad that you left me blank and mysterious. You have a complete collection of characters there on the shelves. There must be a reason why your books sell so well.

ANNACINE

Thank you, Kimberly. They are real for a while.

KIMBERLY

We are all real for a while.

ANNACINE

Are you saying that there is no difference between my creations and Keith's friends?

KIMBERLY

Not as much as you are pouting over.

ANNACINE

Am I pouting? I don't pout.

KIMBERLY

Choose a fancier word if you like. Pouting doesn't work at a certain point in life, and you are past that mile marker. Besides, complaining clashes with the wine. Which is excellent by the way.

ANNACINE

It's odd. I had a car guy in my first book, Check the Brakes. He is unreal now, just like this one you just met, what was his name, Craig? I haven't seen him so he is just a character. Maybe you are on to something.

KIMBERLY

If you drink another glass, I'm afraid that you will be tempted to pull out a Ouija board. And the messages sent to you from it would undoubtedly mirror the mundane dreams you have.

ANNACINE

Enough about me for the moment. You broke up. Again. You are looking for a new ex boyfriend. You spend your time with a writer who sees dead people.

KIMBERLY

If you tell me that I'm dead, I will just die. So I am stuck here with you and have access to a cellar full of wonderful wines. It's a sweet and sour version of the afterlife. I have more than that, so that proves I'm alive.

ANNACINE

What other evidence do you have?

KIMBERLY

Committees, galas, friends. Good friends like you and Keith.

ANNACINE

Are you still studying French with Keith?

KIMBERLY

Yes, you should have joined us.

ANNACINE

I don't like crowds.

KIMBERLY

A dozen people doesn't constitute a crowd. You might reconsider now that we've decided to take private lessons.

ANNACINE

Oh?

KIMBERLY

It's the same in class as everywhere else.

ANNACINE

What happened?

KIMBERLY

You know what I mean. You've seen it yourself. (*pulls out sheet of paper*) Elles se ruent sur lui. That is what the instructor said to me, thinking that I was his...his whatever. I wrote it down, it sounded cool.

ANNACINE

What does that translate to in English. Never mind. Let me guess, my French is rusty but I know Keith. The women throw themselves at him.

KIMBERLY

Even the one who if they were to throw themselves and miss would undoubtedly break a hip. I must be among that small percentage who are immune to Keith.

(*Annacine regards Kimberly doubtfully*)

ANNACINE

Too many aren't, Kimberly. Immunity weakens.

KIMBERLY

He is faithful to you. He loves you.

ANNACINE

Love is fickle, hearts begin to beat at a different rhythm, the pace slows.

KIMBERLY

That is too depressing to publish. Faith remains constant.

ANNACINE

If you say so. Keith is faithful to wealth as much as to my heart. More so, I think

KIMBERLY

He's a member of the good guy tribe. A real saint.

ANNACINE

I've heard that Luxembourg is where angels go to relax on their days off. Do you think that he would like it?

KIMBERLY

You have the time to go there now and find out. After,

ANNACINE

After what?

KIMBERLY

After you make travel arrangements. You know, flights and hotels. This is wonderful, it will give you something to plan other than someone's demise. You should plan it for the Fall, it is so crowded at this time of year.

Annacine Finley, ex-murderess on the grand tour of Europe. Don't even dream of murder while you are there. You've shot your last load. You are firing blanks.

ANNACINE

You are missing the point. My new role is to not fire, blanks or otherwise. I have no desire to visit Europe.

KIMBERLY

I forget that you aren't a man; they are so easily led. You will not stop murdering until you stop murdering. You have all this due (*spreads arm to include their surroundings*) solely to the heaps of dead men you've piled up.

ANNACINE

And one living man to complete it. (*duplicating Kimberly's gesture*)

KIMBERLY

Why have you never killed a woman?

ANNACINE

Does it matter? Where is Keith now I wonder?

KIMBERLY

He's your husband. Some volunteer organization or another, I suppose.

You are truly done? Retired? How difficult is it to pick up a pen, or to slap a few keys on the computer. Even at your age.

ANNACINE

I'm not at my age.

KIMBERLY

What is the origin of this intense crisis if not age? Illness? Its not Keith?

ANNACINE

No.

KIMBERLY

What then?

ANNACINE

What do you mean?

KIMBERLY

What is the reason for your sudden retirement?

ANNACINE

Why did you ask me 'Is it Keith?'

KIMBERLY

No particular reason, Annacine. It was a natural question.

ANNACINE

Is it? Why?

KIMBERLY

You have your stories...

ANNACINE

My writing.

KIMBERLY

You have your writing. And you have Keith. Are you abandoning one to retain the other?

ANNACINE

Who said that I've abandoned either of them?

KIMBERLY

A moment ago, you said that you were giving up stories, oops, your writing.

ANNACINE

I said no such thing. I've simply resigned from Murder, LLC. I can find mayhem elsewhere, in a less violent variety. I am going to switch genres.

KIMBERLY

You're going to become a man? That changes everything that Keith and I have...

ANNACINE

No, Kim. Genre. You need to pay attention in French class.

KIMBERLY

Does Keith know? This is important.

ANNACINE

There must have been men other than Keith in your French class. What were they like?

(*Kimberly shrugs*)

KIMBERLY

Yeah. So?

ANNACINE

Romance.

KIMBERLY

You can kiss that goodbye once you've changed sides. Well, not exactly kiss, it will be too late by then.

ANNACINE

Romance writing.

KIMBERLY

It doesn't sound romantic to me. At least it won't hurt as much as going the other direction. Everything reversed. I won't even drive by myself in England, and here you are flipping... whatever exactly it is that gets flipped. I imagine that you can keep the same hairdresser. It might even save you a few bucks. I wonder if I were to dress as a man whether I'd get a discount?

ANNACINE

I intend to write romance novels.

KIMBERLY

And you need to be a man write romance novels? That doesn't sound fair, or legal. Have you thought about choosing another area, something other than murder or romance?

ANNACINE

That's genre.

KIMBERLY

I call it a bad idea. Your decision is drastic, dramatic. Wait, I have it. Write drama, you can scribble that while wearing high heels. This deserves a drink. To continued womanhood.

ANNACINE

Romance.

KIMBERLY

As a man who used to be a woman. You'll be firing blanks for sure. You won't even be holding a gun. Not a real one. Romantic? Not to this girl.

Its preferrable that you kill this idea as quickly and as coldly as any of your other victims, before you permit a doctor to stitch foreign parts on to your chassis. As I remember, you remain an intact plastic surgeon virgin. More power to you.

It's creepy, like some Frankenstein movie. Have you considered a new category of writing. Oh what do they call it?

ANNACINE

Genre.

KIMBERLY

You're fixated on sex. Romance is not all sex.

ANNACINE

Honestly Kim, you make me laugh on the most somber of occasions.

KIMBERLY

Frankenstein, that reminds me. It is horror, or science fiction. Forget I suggested writing any of that, your upcoming surgery will be an unnecessary combination of both, designed to permanently disfigure a current masterpiece.

ANNACINE

Me? A masterpiece? I suppose that I am. Ok, you win. I will write romance as a woman.

KIMBERLY

You will? You are? That's wonderful. You had me worried, Annacine. These crazy ideas pop into your head and you seize them with open arms. As a friend, I'm telling you, stick to writing and leave living to others.

(*Annacine pensive at that comment*)

ANNACINE

Keith sits on so many boards where he must run into a lot of women. Some of them are undoubtedly bored. Do many of them run into him, do you think? Are they as bored as....

KIMBERLY

As much as Keith is bored? Is that what you were going to say.

ANNACINE

I don't know what I was going to say.

KIMBERLY

You're bored. That much is obvious. And worried. So much worry that you considered changing genders.

ANNACINE

Genre! You really should have kept up with your lessons at the Alliance Française. They teach French correctly.

KIMBERLY

Annacine, Keith is perfectly contented.

ANNACINE

Contentment is the unabridged version of boredom. Contented with whom do you think?

KIMBERLY

With you, silly. There, it's settled. Now tell me where did your thought of romance originate?

ANNACINE

It began with a speeding ticket.

KIMBERLY

Oh, that is so cliché. Really Annacine, a big strong traffic officer?

ANNACINE

Don't be vulgar. I was thinking of it before that and when I convinced Keith to complete my online traffic school class in my place. It freed up time for me to watch an episode of *The Bachelorette.* I feel guilty.

KIMBERLY

You should. You defrauded the state by having Keith impersonate you

ANNACINE

He is so much better and taking tests. Plus, it helps the state get high scores. That must help them with funding somewhere along the line. I understand the concept of civic duty.

KIMBERLY

That is your concept of civic duty? Please don't write any textbooks for students, the schools are bad enough already.

It's still fraud.

ANNACINE

Fraud, schmaud. What I regret is not thanking the policeman for the ticket.

KIMBERLY

The officer who issued you the fine that you didn't pay, because you passed the course you didn't take? It hasn't helped your driving. Auto accidents happen. That explains your dream about ending up at McDonald's late at night. You should have gone in. That is what I would have done. I'd have found the big, handsome policeman inside, waiting to issue me several more, let's call them summonses. With warm cheese drizzled on top.

ANNACINE

Driving was never my strong suit. I can't wait to get a self-driving car. But it has helped my writing.

KIMBERLY

Have you submitted something romantic to your editor?

ANNACINE

Not exactly. But I shall. Soon.

KIMBERLY

You will not stop murdering until you stop murdering.

ANNACINE

You told me that earlier.

KIMBERLY

Craig could become your solo.

ANNACINE

Craig who?

KIMBERLY

Craig Rogue the car guy. He would be your solo.

ANNACINE

I don't need a solo. Keith already passed my driving school test. Haven't you been listening?

KIMBERLY

A romance solo. Talk about listening, jeesh. Your first flight into the world of romance. And when you crash and burn, I will have learned from your mistakes. It will keep you distracted.

ANNACINE

Distracted?

KIMBERLY

Busy. You can use him as romance.

ANNACINE

That's perversion, not romance.

KIMBERLY

Perversion and romance reside in adjacent zip codes. Romance needs clothes, at least in the beginning. Frankly Annacine, your fashion sense is extinct. To be blunt your clothes are atrocious. You need new clothes. Now. I'll be back later and we can dress you as a woman. It will be fun.

ACT I

SCENE 4

(Various articles of clothing are lain across a sofa from which Annacine will select something to wear)

KIMBERLY

Here we are. This is a sample but if you can't find something here, I'll choose for you.

ANNACINE

You sound like my mother.

KIMBERLY

I recommend fewer insults and more action.

ANNACINE

I guess that I should categorize them first.

KIMBERLY

Now you sound like my mother. You are too organized for this activity. Take a deep breath and relax.

ANNACINE

Hmm, this one has no label. Is it from the ultimate exclusive designer? This one is only as big as a label. You didn't rob from your doll collection I hope. This one I would wear if I were single and had two days left to live.

KIMBERLY

You've a bit longer, but go for it.

ANNACINE

And this one is wonderful if I were already dead, and you were deciding my forever outfit. It has 'Send me straight to hell' written all over it. I must inform Keith that you are not to be involved in my funeral arrangements.

KIMBERLY

What are friends for?

ANNACINE

This top truly would be happier buried in an unmarked grave. Have you actually worn any of these alleged articles of clothing?

KIMBERLY

Certainly.

ANNACINE

In public?

KIMBERLY

In Lexington.

ANNACINE

That fleshpot? Lexington explains many of these....items. Wait now, I may have spoken in haste. This one is fine, appropriate for Sunday worship; if you are into some alien-based cult its perfect.

KIMBERLY

We all have secrets.

ANNACINE

Just when you think that you know someone. Now this one, I like it. This top is a joke, isn't it? You added this one on purpose, expecting me to select it. It's a plant. By the way, have you noticed that hideous plant? Keith brought it home. It goes with your Invasion of the body snatchers silky thing..

I like it. But knowing that you offered it to me as a drab, safe, bet, I should pass. But then, you would expect me to pass, and select one of your other tops. It's a double bluff.

KIMBERLY

Pick a simple top to wear to a bar to talk to a few men as research for your foray into romance. You are not being fitted for a wedding gown.

ANNACINE

Does Keith love me?

KIMBERLY

Wow, where did that come from? Keith loves you.

ANNACINE

You say it so matter of factly.

KIMBERLY

It is a matter of fact.

ANNACINE

Kimberly, I'm anxious. I am so very anxious. I've known what to do, I saw clearly what I was going to do, for the past twenty odd years. At this moment, with you, selecting a top seems to be the most frightening event ever.

KIMBERLY

You could go topless, none of the patrons at the Willow would treat that as a fearful event. They would be all atwitter.

ANNACINE

I do like this one. But, oh the heck with it (*rips it slightly to increase the exposure it offers*). There, perfect. All it needed was a slut adjustment. I meant slight adjustment. All the girls are doing it.

KIMBERLY

Girls, yes. And now for shoes.

ANNACINE

Men don't look at shoes. Keith never does, and oh, I hope that Craig is not one of those foot fetishers you read about. He is an excellent prospect in all other aspects.

KIMBERLY

And now to sitting.

ANNACINE

I'm exhausted.

KIMBERLY

You can't collapse onto a bar stool.

ANNACINE

What if I collapse into a man? Will he catch me?

KIMBERLY

At your age, it won't be romantic, but more likely a Medicare claim.

Keith says I will be forever 23 years old.

KIMBERLY

Then you shall be.

ANNACINE

Keith is preoccupied. He is always occupied, but this is different. Do you notice a change in him? You and he are on boards together.

KIMBERLY

That's all. We are on boards together. You know what it boards are like.

ANNACINE

I don't. I serve on no boards. When he talks to me about the boards you serve on, it reminds me of my younger brother and the neighbor tomboy who was his closest companion. You are his little tomboy.

KIMBERLY

A tomboy? That is a dagger to my female heart.

ANNACINE

No boards for me. I leave it to my work to speak for me. Keith has changed, I don't recognize him.

KIMBERLY

Is the change in Keith or yourself?

ANNACINE

I asked myself that question so often that I no longer know which answer is true.

KIMBERLY

Maybe neither is true.

ANNACINE

Keith is more preoccupied.

KIMBERLY

He is a busy man with his boards and his tomboy.

ANNACINE

He has become secretive and is spending more time out of the house. He claims to be fixing up the DeSoto, but a year ago he would have performed the work himself instead of outsourcing it.

KIMBERLY

You would not have met Craig if he hadn't.

ANNACINE

There has been no increase in calls.

KIMBERLY

From Craig?

ANNACINE

No, Kimberly. To Keith. At the same time, he is more attentive when he is in the house.

KIMBERLY

Craig?

ANNACINE

Keith. Kimberly, I have not met Craig; you have. Are you sure he is not an imaginary friend? Remember that your fantasy is not my reality. I'm a writer so it goes the other direction. Besides, this vaporous Craig is not the only candidate that I can audition.

KIMBERLY

Can you name another? No, I didn't think so. You two must meet. As for Keith's preoccupation and super attentiveness, it may be the same amount of attention, spread over fewer hours so it only appears heightened. How long has this been going on?

ANNACINE

A month, six weeks?

KIMBERLY

Not more?

ANNACINE

I'm not sure. I don't think that Keith has behaved this way more than six weeks. Why? Is it important? It was about six weeks agon that I mentioned romance in passing. It was an idle phrase, nothing more.

KIMBERLY

Men of a certain age.

ANNACINE

No, not that sort of romance. My romance.

KIMBERLY

It must be nice to have your own romance. Is there more than one variety? Here I thought myself blessed to have all of these magnificent tops. Which one best accentuates my tomboyishness?

ANNACINE

I should have said nothing to him about my desire to write romance novels. He's worried about it. That is why he is having this work done on the DeSoto. He mentioned nothing about it, as if I am blind. He is going to sell it, I can just feel it. The car has been with us since the beginning, and now. We can have both, the old and the new. Don't say a word to Keith about my new writing style. I will tell him later. This must be a surprise. That's romantic. Isn't it? I will bring up the subject after our anniversary.

(*Kimberly nods*)

I can have both.

KIMBERLY

The old and the new?

ANNACINE

Keith. And Craig. Murder and romance. Murderers make the most intriguing story tellers.

KIMBERLY

Does it apply the other way round?

ANNACINE

How is that?

KIMBERLY

On your feet. You need to show me how you move, how you can lower your voice to force men to lean in. Hell, they want to lean in anyway. One loosened button is worth five hundred dollars in voice lessons.

ANNACINE

How is this? Rumor has it that

KIMBERLY

You're rusty, Annacine. Husky is effective. Trust me. I will be your sexidor.

ANNACINE

Sexidor? There is no such word.

KIMBERLY

But genre exists?

ANNACINE

There you said it.

KIMBERLY

Whoop de do. At the Willow you will hear words that aren't in your Sunday school dictionary. Sexidor, agreed?

ANNACINE

I agree.

KIMBERLY

Think of it as I'm like Sherlock Holmes, the world's first consulting private sexidor.

ANNACINE

My life is complete.

KIMBERLY

Listen to me and it will be, soon.

Willow wolves will watch you the way the way that you used to watch them when your stalked them as murderers and victims.

ANNACINE

Like this? (*Intense gaze*) I call it my je ne sais quoi.

KIMBERLY

Lose it.

ANNACINE

You don't even know what it is?

KIMBERLY

Your je ne sais quoi.

ANNACINE

Well, yes. You said that rather well.

KIMBERLY

You know that I have been taking French classes. I may be traveling overseas soon.

ANNACINE

Why didn't I know this, Kimberly. It seems sudden, mysterious. With whom?

KIMBERLY

I'll find someone. I call it romantic. Let's return to the wolves. Your je ne sais quoi look.

ANNACINE

This one? It's my magic.

KIMBERLY

You need to leave your je ne sais quoi here at home. Hide it in a far corner of a closet along with any talk of magic. There may be a full moon tomorrow but you won't be decorating it with any unnecessary ornaments. I want you to appear normal.

ANNACINE

(*Sighs*)

KIMBERLY

But very seductive. Men are sensitive to creepiness. Alcohol reduces their acuity, but we will be there early enough that they will detect any je ne sais quoi you are wearing. Creepiness is two levels beyond normal woman crazy. Have fun. A woman must be joyful until that last moment.

ANNACINE

Which moment?

KIMBERLY

The final moment.

ANNACINE

When the book is done? My book is nothing more than a dream, like romance itself, with the characters milling around, waiting to be heard and to be assigned words to speak. I have yet to convince them to buy into my dreams, dreams as worthless as bitcoin.

KIMBERLY

Forget the book for now. It can write itself afterwards.

ACT I

SCENE 5

(Kimberly and Keith phase in and out of their characters' characters)

(*In secondary character*)

KIMBERLY

What will you tell the police?

KEITH

It must have been brake failure. The lines were just replaced, but they were defective.

KIMBERLY

Good. The police will be unable to disbelieve you. The perfect husband. I admire how you excel at honesty and kindness.

KEITH

Kindness is a curse. The kinder one is, the more intensely resentment reflects back. Crudeness is an infinitely more precious gift. Tell me honestly, does she suspect anything?

KIMBERLY

Your wife?

KEITH

She has been acting strange lately. But then so have I. We've been so circumspect. Famous last words. I sense that she is deliberately taunting me, offering me even more reason to do what we are planning. You're her friend, what is your opinion?

KIMBERLY

You are finally paying attention to the woman you are about to murder. It is too late for regrets, my dear.

KEITH

This is different. I am different.

KIMBERLY

You are wrong, darling. Men are decisive. Don't Hamlet me.

KEITH

What does that even mean?

KIMBERLY

We are not performing Hamlet. It's a simple murder. Your hands won't be soiled. It is not a crime, only an accident. It won't be dramatic.

KEITH

It won't be dramatic?

KIMBERLY

You understand my words perfectly well.

KEITH

I'm not sure, my love. Not dramatic for you. Not for me. Maybe not. It is all just words. For us. But for my wife.

KIMBERLY

Envision your wife already dead. She is dead. Live, die. simple. C'est simple comme bonjour. Or au revoir. You've read the writing on the wall, we both have.

(*In primary character*)

KEITH

I need a break.

KIMBERLY

A break. That's rich.

KEITH

I chose poorly with Craig. He is too..

KIMBERLY

He is that.

KEITH

He is not your type. If I'd known that Craig was going to collect women like a greasy kitten, I'd have done the restoration myself.

KIMBERLY

A greasy kitten?

KEITH

Annacine is the writer, not me. She has a way with words that Craig

KIMBERLY

The greasy kitten

KEITH

That Craig has with women.

KIMBERLY

That he has with some women. Some of us are immune. Me, I've always been sickly.

KEITH

Immunity is ominous. This scheme is complex amd your tone and twinkling eyes combine to worry me. Have you devised an additional that will materialize at some unfortunate and unexpected time.

KIMBERLY

Like an accident involving faulty breaks or a surprise character in Annacine's books?

KEITH

Clever women are bad enough, but I have come to accept them.

KIMBERLY

That is very manly of you.

KEITH

They can't help flaunting it however. I suppose that you won't tell me.

KIMBERLY

Your make intuition has not divined it? Now that you mention it, a greasy kitten does evoke a certain image. You want to cuddle him after having cleaned him from tip to tip.

KEITH

The shower is in there if you need to cool off, Kimberly.

KIMBERLY

I'm familiar with the route. I've been over here often enough. What is he like?

KEITH

He enjoys cars. That is why I hired him.

KIMBERLY

Not what does he like, but what is he like?

KEITH

Haven't you had enough boyfriends?

KIMBERLY

How many are in two enoughs?

KEITH

One too many, Kimberly. We agreed to do this project on the condition that there were to be no new boyfriends for you. I have that role now.

KIMBERLY

No greasy kitten?

KEITH

Craig has no part in this plot of ours. Ok, back to work.

(*In secondary character*)

There is no crime, only an accident.

KIMBERLY

Will the car be ready?

KEITH

I need him to focus.

KIMBERLY

And I need you to focus. There can only be one queen. No harem for you, this other woman has scruples. Despite what you read in the news, morals aren't extinct.

KEITH

My wife...

KIMBERLY

Your wife this and your wife that. Stop it. The time has come to excise her from the story. It is inevitable that she dies. The sooner she is gone, the longer we can live together.

KEITH

You are an Eve. My dear.

KIMBERLY

If not for Eve, Adam would be an uneducated, unpaid gardener. No beautiful home for him, no other woman for him.

KEITH

Why does it come always to the man to act?

KIMBERLY

It is nature's way.

Is it nature's curiosity that drives to see how much pressure a man can endure?

KIMBERLY

I confess that it is my favorite sport. I don't tire of it.

KEITH

Women tire of nothing.

KIMBERLY

Kimberly kisses Keith.

(*In primary character*)

KEITH

This is not yet part of the script, Kimberly.

KIMBERLY

You need to kiss me, here, on this couch, now.

KEITH

I know but

KIMBERLY

This was your idea, your words, your promise. You twisted her words against her. This was your vow to me. Is it still your promise? Kiss me now or this entire scheme collapses. There can be no second chances. Don't let lack of talent deter you. Believe in yourself and much as I believe in you.

KEITH

(*approaches Kimberly to take her in his arms, kisses her lightly, just as the door jostles*)

KEITH

Stop for a moment. I hear something. (*kiss is broken, door opens, Rachel enters*)

What are you doing here?

RACHEL

(*crosses room and lifts the potted plant*)

I am here to dig things up you might say. Stevie deserves better. I arrived in the nick of time, Stevie doesn't look well. (*exits*)

KIMBERLY

Who the heck is Stevie?

KEITH

For some unknown reason, I believe that I know the answer. But I wish to Heaven that I did not.

KIMBERLY

What shall we do?

KEITH

What shall I do? Is that your question? I'll take care of her, soon. I don't have time rehearse this part.

KIMBERLY

Soon needs to be soon, Keith. This entire undertaking will collapse if nosey Nellie

KEITH

Rachel.

KIMBERLY

If rambling Rachel opens her mouth.

KEITH

She never closes it.

KIMBERLY

Soon Keith, soon. If not soon, then what value is any of this?

We are not performing a comedy here. Kiss me. I'm not your aunt at the family reunion. If you really want this you must make it real. Otherwise, it will rupture like cheap tin instead of the hardened steel required. Which it is? Steel or

KEITH

(*Keith kisses Kimberly*)

You've changed your lipstick color.

KIMBERLY

No, I haven't. I like red.

KEITH

Not pale pink? Rachel likely noticed.

KIMBERLY

I don't wear pale pink; I leave that to Annacine. It's part of her new

KEITH

Her new what?

KIMBERLY

Sense of fashion, and newfound

KEITH

Passion?

KIMBERLY

Fashion. She is happy with it.

KEITH

Is she? Happy I mean.

KIMBERLY

More or less. You know, I've been thinking about them brakes.

KEITH

Them brakes. That is what Craig calls them.

KIMBERLY

Is it now?

ACT II

SCENE 1

(Annacine practicing her walk, with a glass of wine in hand)

ANNACINE

Quack, quack, quack. It's a waddle, not a sway, Annacine. Prisoners on death row move more gracefully. Perhaps one of my books will help. *Cutting Edges on the Catwalk.* Perfect. (attempts are more or less unsuccessful)

(Knock at door from garage. Annacine scurries to couch and relaxes just in time as Craig enters from garage)

ANNACINE

Hey! Who are you? If you are...

CRAIG

My name is Craig Rogue. I am doing some work for Keith Finley. You must be Annacine. Hello. I hope you don't mind me stepping in unannounced. But Keith said that if I needed something, to stop by. I drove over to root through the garage. Each man has his own unique non system of organization. You know, various parts, bulbs, extra floor mats. He has a lot of stuff. I apologize if I am interrupting.

ANNACINE

Craig? Kimberly Fredrichs told me about you.

CRAIG

I doubt she knows me well enough to tell you much.

ANNACINE

Well enough.

CRAIG

Am I interrupting you?

ANNACINE

I was just sitting here, thinking that I need to practice.

CRAIG

Practice your writing?

ANNACINE

In a way. Strange, but I haven't practiced in a long time.

CRAIG

It is the same for a car. They need to be driven occasionally.

ANNACINE

Even older cars?

CRAIG

Older cars in particular. It keeps them younger, you might say, more supple and ready to roar down the road.

ANNACINE

I see. That sounds like good advice. Have you shared it with Keith?

CRAIG

I'm sure that he knows. He's had her for a long time.

ANNACINE

I wouldn't say that.

CRAIG

Keith told me that the car has been with him since the beginning.

ANNACINE

The beginning of what? Did he say?

CRAIG

He didn't tell me exactly, just that he had owned it for decades.

ANNACINE

It was mine, before it was his. Some women do that, they offer their prize possession to men.

CRAIG

Like a dowry? I've heard of that tradition in some cultures.

ANNACINE

What do you need Craig?

CRAIG

Nothing really. I just had my hands buried in parts.

ANNACINE

Which parts would those be?

CRAIG

Some brushes for a generator; they provide a spark, and some new brake shoes, sized just right so that they don't overheat. Boring stuff like that.

ANNACINE

I didn't realize that simple parts could be so tantalizing.

CRAIG

I enjoy them. After fussing around, I finished, and came in here to wash my hands. (*Notices book on the floor*). Are you working on a new book? Keith said that these were all yours. Murder mysteries he told me.

ANNACINE

That has been my genre, yes.

CRAIG

How do you do that? Write all the time, I mean? Do you have to become your character?

ANNACINE

That helps. (*Annacine gets in character*)

I used to write in pen, and that seemed more real, my hands smeared in ink. As yours are smeared with, whatever. Let me see them.

CRAIG

What?

ANNACINE

Your hands. Let me see them. She approaches and he turns them over, displaying the palms. Here, hold this, passing him her wine glass. He holds it by the globe, not the handle.

(*She grabs his free hand in hers.*)

So strong and powerful, smeared with,

CRAIG

Dust and grime, sorry. I've marked your glass.

ANNACINE

The proof of your labor. I should write that down. Yet I have no doubt that I will recall vividly this conversation.

Oh Craig. You are doing so much for Keith, getting the DeSoto restored. On his behalf you are dirtying your strong hands in the process. And my hands, unmarked, the blood washed away, while yours show honest efforts of repair and good works. One sip. I'm not asking you to rev an engine, simply have a glass of wine.

CRAIG

I'm driving.

ANNACINE

A sip then. It's not poisoned, you can see my lipstick here. Shall I pivot it for you? I've been told that I am a wonderful pivoter. Here sip, it's wine, fine wine, like fine women it requires no added aphrodisiac.

CRAIG

It's not yet noon, Annacine.

(*Annacine blushes, takes the glass from him, sips from it and sets it down, releases Craig's hand.*)

Do you care to know the time? This is an old watch, a gift from, never mind from whom. It reads eleven o'clock twice a day, each time twice a day. Isn't that clever, like being able to redo each moment of one's life. Or if one is dissatisfied, poof, one just jumps ahead 12 hours, no jet lag. It's 11 pm, time magnificent for a first or final glass of wine.

CRAIG

One sip then I must leave.

ANNACINE

Craig, I'm curious about the car.

CRAIG

The DeSoto?

ANNACINE

Yes, I know about the DeSoto. I'm surprised that Keith is putting so much effort into that old car.

CRAIG

He is?

ANNACINE

Well, you are. Keith drives it 5 minutes a year. Oh alright, a few times per year. I'm not sure how safe it is for any trips.

CRAIG

It will be in perfect operating condition when I am through with it. Soon, a week or so. Parts have been available, although original brakes are nearly impossible to find. But there are good aftermarket ones.

ANNACINE

Is he going to sell the DeSoto?

Why is Keith doing this now? If he were to sell it, it would just kill me.

Is he going to sell the DeSoto?

CRAIG

He hasn't mentioned anything to me about selling the car.

ANNACINE

But he could if he wanted to? Easily, I mean.

CRAIG

Absolutely. I'd buy it myself if the price were right.

ANNACINE

You would? You would step in and take his place?

CRAIG

Er? His place?

ANNACINE

Sorry. I misspoke. The car, you would buy it? But why would he sell it? Its more than a car to us, it's a good luck charm, after market brakes at all. It is like a pet who never dies, a small meaningless gift from our first Christmas together. I can't imagine our life together without it. Silly, I suppose?

CRAIG

I can see now where you find the passion to murder perfect strangers.

ANNACINE

Is he going to sell it?

CRAIG

I don't think so, Annacine. That would be foolish. (*finally drinks*) I must go. Thank you for the wine. Oh, I meant to compliment you on your shoes. They are very stylish.

ANNACINE

I hope we meet again. (*Craig nods and exits*)

Annacine goes to bookshelf, accidently kicking book along the way,

I've kicked the murder habit, you must return to where you belong. I have found a new idol in romance. A newish life.

Lights several matches in succession.

Life, ready to spring forward. This one, yet unborn, expectant, waiting, unborn. And once born, preparing to die. A flame, a short burning and then, a puff of random circumstance (*blows out match*), an unforeseen accident (*drops second match in wine*). My venture into romance begins, surrounded by an atmosphere of death. This romance is work.

New deities demand new rituals. (*puts glass on bookshelf and exits*)

Those with the saddest of lives are condemned to live the longest she read from the cover of one of her earlier books what is stupid thing to say but what do you expect from a publisher who poisoned himself at the age of 35 she reached the line again
putrid perfumed to profound. she removes the dust jacket and throws it in the garbage there is life and death and nothing more.

ACT II

SCENE 2

ANNACINE

All that I can say is we survived it.

KIMBERLY

I'm proud of you, Annacine. You actually spoke with a few men without any obvious indications that you were plotting a gruesome death for any of them.

ANNACINE

I felt like a defanged lioness.

KIMBERLY

Believe me when I tell you that it did not show. If anything, you came across as a gazelle. I told you before we left for the Willow that men are sensitive to creepiness.

ANNACINE

A gazelle is more vulnerable than a toothless cat.

KIMBERLY

You demanded to be let into this game. Just because you are on the court doesn't give you the right to change the rules. Artists are expected to sacrifice themselves for their art.

ANNACINE

Don't mock it, Kimberly.

KIMBERLY

I'm not. Enjoy the thrill of the hunt from the perspective of the prey.

ANNACINE

None of my victims enjoyed being killed.

KIMBERLY

We are not discussing murder. Although you may find yourself devoured, nonetheless. Admit it, you found it exciting, a game where no one is expected to die.

ANNACINE

Strange drinks offered by unknown men in darkened bars is not my idea of romance.

KIMBERLY

It was a start. Consider it a practice run. You should thank me for sacrificing a precious evening for a late bloomer like you. Unfortunately, you don't have the time, or the aptitude to really excel. The things that I do for a friend.

ANNACINE

I am grateful, truly I am. I appreciate the male touches that you absorbed like a football player blocking

KIMBERLY

I was running interference for you.

ANNACINE

You generated so much interference, that the evening was nearly signal free for me. It struck me that you instigated the majority of advances

KIMBERLY

Advances? I hope you don't use terms like that in your first romance. Unless you are setting it in the era of slowly removed bonnets and tumbling hair. Am I making you blush?

I told you before we set foot in the first establishment, that the choice of seat, at a table or at the bar was only the first step. Your walk, the way you sat yourself, the mingling of your perfume and a man's cologne would rank as a contest of pheromones.

Aren't you going to take any notes, Annacine?

ANNACINE

I committed your monologue to memory the first time you told me this foolishness. I may use it one day when it's a choice between having nothing of value to write and suicide.

KIMBERLY

Oh good, just as long as it is in your memory. The nearly imperceptible delay as minds register your arrival, the hush as they take your measure and consider their options.

ANNACINE

It reminds me of TSA at the airport when you don't have pre-check.

KIMBERLY

Romance requires rehearsal. I'm serious, Annacine.

ANNACINE

So am I.

KIMBERLY

And in this site of smoldering passion, where only the most melancholic of music was appropriate, you crushed the ambience before a romantic word was uttered, by parting your moistened, red lips and nearly shouting, 'Chardonnay, please.'

ANNACINE

What was wrong with ordering a Chardonnay?

KIMBERLY

Chardonnay is drab. You'd have been better off ordering a beer and whacking the nearest man. That would have been a better conversation starter. You could have broken the ice by breaking a neck.

ANNACINE

I wish I had. I was nervous, and I thought, it has been so long, nearly a month,

KIMBERLY

Nearly a month?

ANNACINE

Nearly I month since I killed someone. I had an urge...

KIMBERLY

I can't blame Keith for spending so much time with others. I'm kidding, Annacine. We have a great deal of work before us. Three weeks without blood, like some sort of vampiric wordsmith. You may not have time left to satisfy your thirst before

ANNACINE

Before what?

KIMBERLY

I don't know. Before you reoffend? Who knows how much time any of us have?

ANNACINE

What should I have done?

KIMBERLY

You should have followed my lead.

ANNACINE

I was nervous. I reasoned that if I didn't do as you did, one of us would remain free to post bail.

KIMBERLY

The next time ask the bartender or a neighbor what they suggest. It opens the door to conversation. And a free first drink.

ANNACINE

Free drinks are never free. I remember that from.

KIMBERLY

From where?

ANNACINE

From another life.

KIMBERLY

I can't picture you having had another life. That last comment, combined with your apparent firsthand knowledge of being bailed out, revises my opinion of sweet murderous Annacine. That is romantic.

Free drinks are never free. But they are often worth the price.

ANNACINE

I'm not sure if romance is for me.

KIMBERLY

Ok.

ANNACINE

OK?

KIMBERLY

If you want to give up, fine. The future is not for everyone.

ANNACINE

I'm not giving up anything.

KIMBERLY

You are. That's my opinion. I'm not forcing you to convert to anything, Annacine.

ANNACINE

Some friend you are! This is irritating.

KIMBERLY

Irritability is a sign of withdrawal.

ANNACINE

I could smack you. That would make me feel better.

KIMBERLY

Then you would feel worse, you recidivist.

ANNACINE

True.

KIMBERLY

I don't see why you need to do any of this research. Did you kill anyone as preparation for writing your first book? Think before you answer. I really don't want to spend money on an outfit to wear to a trial. Those sorts of clothes are single use only.

ANNACINE

No, I did not murder anyone as research. I discussed the plot with Keith, and no he did not murder anyone either. Murder is not in his nature. Keith read my drafts and reacted to the story as a normal reader would. He didn't like the ending, and maybe he was right, but I went with what I wrote.

KIMBERLY

You could do the same with romance.

ANNACINE

And then I caved. I deferred to Keith, not because he was my husband, that is the truth. I didn't change the end, not for that reason, but because he had read it. It was as if I bore it while he delivered it. Does that make sense? (*no response*)

Have you noticed that the plant is gone?

KIMBERLY

Keith mentioned that he was going to take care of her, I mean it. You've got me assigning genders to everything, Annacine.

ANNACINE

It wasn't Keith. Tell me, how did I perform last night? A glass of wine before you pass sentence on my passionless romantic crimes?

KIMBERLY

Please, no wine. After last night I am prepared to reinstate prohibition.

ANNACINE

How about lemonade? I have a fresh pitcher in the fridge.

(*exits to kitchen*)

Keith belongs to more boards than I can imagine! How does he manage it?

KIMBERLY

He excels at juggling.

ANNACINE

And more? I must join a board. You disagree?

KIMBERLY

No.

ANNACINE

But? (*returns with lemonade*

KIMBERLY

Will you have time? You told me that you are moving to romance. Why? If you can't answer immediately, you have no valid response.

ANNACINE

I

KIMBERLY

Replies that begin with I are the worst. I is the most overrated word in the English language. The world would be a better place if we excised the I word along with the F word.

ANNACINE

Boredom. Finding interesting people and inventing more and more intricate methods to extinguish them is tedious. Boredom.

KIMBERLY

That's a good word. It's not great, but truthful.

ANNACINE

I considered joining one of Keith's boards.

KIMBERLY

Boards are incapable of solving boredom.

ANNACINE

Hmm. He might consider that encroachment.

KIMBERLY

What are you? A UN peacekeeper? You're his wife. Is sharing his bed encroaching? If you are asking my opinion, I have none. I'm exhausted. I'm depleted.

ANNACINE

So am I. (*fills glass*) You can agree that I'm bored.

KIMBERLY

You're bored. That's understandable, Annacine. You have a wonderful life, adoring fans, an equally adoring husband, an adorable house. You are so adored; you should move into a cathedral. They are constantly in need of renovation, and you have the exact amount of boredom to carry it off. You might even be able to push someone from the roof during repairs, or have a chandelier fall on a dignitary. Do churches have chandeliers? If not, they should. Yes, a murder in a cathedral. You could jot out a novel in the time it takes to paint one inside wall. I've given you the idea, even a title, Murder in the Cathedral.

ANNACINE

It's been done.

KIMBERLY

Oh.

ANNACINE

Do you ever have the same dream?

KIMBERLY

The same dream as you? How would I know?

ANNACINE

The same dream that you've experienced several times before?

KIMBERLY

Why yes. Don't we all?

ANNACINE

I've come to realize that the same repetition occurs in real life. Yet with the sun high in the sky and eyes wide open, the repeats are worse to watch. I can't shake myself awake, or to rely on a full bladder to stir you away.

KIMBERLY

That reminds me..

ANNACINE

That you need to tinkle?

KIMBERLY

That I need to fill my glass if I am to have any hope of a full bladder Don't you just hate depletion? Life repeats Annacine. Repeats are ok. They are gifts, not tedious reruns.

ANNACINE

Will you go with me again?

KIMBERLY

To a place like last night? What are you, nineteen?

ANNACINE

I wish.

KIMBERLY

You do?

ANNACINE

This is all so renew to me.

KIMBERLY

Renew?

ANNACINE

I'm rusty. You are so effective at critiquing me. May I critique you as well?

KIMBERLY

Maybe later. I do it well enough myself. Listen Annacine.

My crisis was at twenty-five. I remember that my parents were so proud that I was still precocious. I found that strange as my ex accused me of that as well.

ANNACINE

Precocious? Or promiscuous?

KIMBERLY

It could have been. By that point, I was no longer listening to him.

ANNACINE

Your ex-husband?

KIMBERLY

Let's stick with X, I lump all the double x people as x or soon to be x.

ANNACINE

Men can be so cruel when they have truth on their side

KIMBERLY

That proves how weak they are.

ANNACINE

Does it?

KIMBERLY

Women don't require facts in order to be cruel. You don't believe me, Annacine?

ANNACINE

I've never thought of men and women from that perspective.

KIMBERLY

You've written from that perspective a dozen times. More than a few. Am I right?

ANNACINE

I guess so. No. I don't understand. Let's start this discussion over. You have read a dozen of my sixty-two books?

KIMBERLY

I've read one of your mysteries a dozen times.

ANNACINE

You must love it. Which one?

KIMBERLY

Does it matter? The first I think. They are all the same.

ANNACINE

If you've only read a dozen, er, one a dozen times, how can you say that they are no different, one from another?

KIMBERLY

They are bestsellers. It stands to reason that they are the same.

ANNACINE

That hurts, Kimberly. My books are absolutely not clones.

KIMBERLY

They are to me, Annacine. I never figure out who did it. They are insoluble problems. I hate them

ANNACINE

Oh, thank you, dear Kimberly. Insoluble problems! That was precisely my intent

KIMBERLY

I'm tired of discussing the written word. Can we please return to real life? I dated a much younger man recently.

ANNACINE

Have you no shame?

KIMBERLY

I got rid of it. I dug a small hole, you would be amazed at how tiny shame can be and buried it in the darkest shade I could find.

He was nice, but he told me that he was visiting churches hoping to spot God at one of his "known hangouts" was how he phrased it.

ANNACINE

I don't understand men, young or old.

KIMBERLY

You try too hard. It only works if you don't think of them as complete people, but more as hairy children with different if equally sized appetites

ANNACINE

How young was he? Was he sweet?

KIMBERLY

Annacine!

ANNACINE

It is research.

KIMBERLY

Men have thrown that line to me so often that I bought a white coat for protection.

ANNACINE

I will have to reflect on what that means later. And the boy?

KIMBERLY

He was a young man, Annacine. I obey some laws, you know. Speaking of dreams, Craig looked dreamy last evening. Fine as wine in the subdued lighting.

ANNACINE

I thought you had too much wine.

KIMBERLY

Little else interests me. Men and wine mesh so well. You use one bottle to attract him, another to break up and a third to forget him. Good things come in threes. Afterwards, you buy a new outfit. I call it nature's cycle.

ANNACINE

Alcohol certainly fertilizes the wit.

KIMBERLY

Shakespeare?

ANNACINE

One hundred percent Finley. I write best sellers you know.

KIMBERLY

And you've elected to chuck it all.

ANNACINE

Chucking all is more in your wheelhouse.

KIMBERLY

Romance is in my blood. I sense it pulsing, streaming through, round and round, a crimson throbbing propelled by my heart's powerful pump.

ANNACINE

See your cardiologist.

KIMBERLY

All that you require is a blood transfusion. Figuratively speaking. Romance resides in each of us. A tiny touch of direction, my experience guiding you to new heights.

ANNACINE

Which heights?

KIMBERLY

Is it the height of luxury or the lap of luxury? I am not blessed like you, living in this palace, cocooned in this lap of luxury.

ANNACINE

All of this was not a gift. I worked for it. That gives it an exquisitely sweeter taste. Are you jealous?

KIMBERLY

Jealousy? My boyfriends suffer it, not I. I manage to live within my means as deliciously as you do within yours. You have your lap of luxury and I pursue the luxury of laps.

ANNACINE

You are incorrigible Kimberly.

KIMBERLY

It is not Kimberly who is changing genders.

ANNACINE

Stop it.

KIMBERLY

So should you. I tell in all honesty that I cannot be friends with a man. Especially you who knows me too well.

ANNACINE

Well enough to recognize when you are joking.

KIMBERLY

Is this lemonade spiked? If not, it should be.

ANNACINE

I have been having weird dreams, Kimberly. Violent images that in the past I would have translated into bestsellers. Now they haunt me. They are first person, targeted directly at me. They are so unlike their predecessors.

KIMBERLY

Tell me.

ANNACINE

You will laugh.

KIMBERLY

I laugh at life, not dreams.

ANNACINE

You can be annoyingly cavalier at times.

KIMBERLY

Men find shallowness among my best qualities. I could have been a successful character for you. Readers love honesty.

ANNACINE

They prefer villains.

KIMBERLY

Like Craig. Did you see him last night? A rogue named Rogue.

ANNACINE

(*Annacine pours herself lemonade*)
Yes, again. I met him the other day here at the house when he stopped by to pick up some parts.

KIMBERLY

You did! I mean you did? You didn't mention this earlier.

ANNACINE

It was just some parts. It was a brief encounter.

KIMBERLY

Yet one mention his name and you reach for an ice pack. Drink up before you overheat, again. Or is it too late?

ANNACINE

You're one to talk. (*sips*). See, I'm not gulping.

KIMBERLY

If you took him under your wing, you could write a romance novel together. Another few encounters might generate a real turn pager.
(*Annacine guzzles her lemonade*)

Passion is quicker than the fastest writer.

ANNACINE

Where did that come from?

KIMBERLY

I must have read it in your People magazine interview.

ANNACINE

Did I say that? Someone must have made that up. I wish I had said a phrase as pithy.

KIMBERLY

You do? You also said murder is life's passion distilled.

ANNACINE

I did? I wish I had said such beautiful words.

KIMBERLY

Say it again at your next interview, and who could contest them in the future..

ANNACINE

That would not be honest.

KIMBERLY

Passion has nothing to do with being correct.

ANNACINE

You did it again Kimberly.

KIMBERLY

I'll zip my lips. The weather is nice. It's positively passionate. What did you put in this lemonade?

ANNACINE

The usual; water, lemons, vodka.

KIMBERLY

Vodka? Is that why Russian authors are so good? Vodka and ink mix well. Who knew. Vodka. Are you trying to imbibe me? I leave that pleasure to men.

ANNACINE

One at a time?

KIMBERLY

Seriously, Annacine, how is your switch progressing?

ANNACINE

I'll be truthful.

KIMBERLY

That's no fun. Life is best when lying.

ANNACINE

Stop upstaging me, else I will be forced to murder you.

KIMBERLY

If you only knew.

ANNACINE

What?

KIMBERLY

You've converted to the other side. I looked that word up later, you know.

Genre. Specifically, the romance genre. It's all Lifetime and that other channel. Cinderellas and yoga. Not that chair yoga for

ANNACINE

For?

KIMBERLY

For older women. Women older than either of us. Much older. Romance is a healthy echo of passion.

ANNACINE

If you are going to continue to speak my unwritten lines, you're going to force me to fetch a revolver and end my competitor. There is nothing wrong with romance at any age. I want to explore new senses, emotions, unique and fresh scents.

KIMBERLY

Bravo.

ANNACINE

My friend Rachel encouraged me to buy scented candles and visit the zoo.

KIMBERLY

Why the zoo?

ANNACINE

I have no idea. Rachel has her world that she carries around with her, inhaling it from it periodically like one of those electronic cigarettes. In this case, like so many others, her advice did not sound very useful, so I did not ask for details. Her exact words were 'If you visit the zoo, go all out and take your candles along. You won't regret it.'

KIMBERLY

Ok. I don't know about the zoo, but as far as going to see some wildlife not behind bars, but in bars, let's have a few more lessons in the wilds of Oldham county, and if you are still uncomfortable, we will go to plan B.

ANNACINE

What is Plan B?

KIMBERLY

Plan B is in development.

ANNACINE

That might work. You are a good friend, Kimberly. I'd still like to smack you, though.

ACT II

SCENE 3

(Poker night)

CHUCK

I'm out.

GENE

Out? Out as in out?

CHUCK

I'm out.

KEITH

You don't usually lose this quickly.

CHUCK

And you don't usually invite someone who can play poker. Thanks for filling in, Craig.

GENE

What did you say happened to Wilson, Keith?

KEITH

Tonight is his wife's birthday.

GENE

If he had been here tonight, he'd have spent less money. And I would have a birthday gift instead.

CRAIG

Is today your birthday? There is a lot of that going around this month.

GENE

No, it is not my birthday. I'm just saying that I'd be better off if Wilson had skipped the party and played with us tonight.

CHUCK

Oh, the delusions of the single man.

GENE

I can at least play poker. Hey, you are as single as I am.

CHUCK

There is a difference between us.

CRAIG

Other than the gap in your skill at cards?

GENE

Chuck always crashes and burns. Tonight's castasrophe was more spectacular than I've experienced in the past. Are you taking lessons, Chuck? If so, demand a refund.

CHUCK

I am an observant single man, Craig. While Gene here is a poker maestro, except when someone like you sits in. I pay attention in both games. (*confusion*). In life and in poker I pay attention to the game and to the players. While you Gene, only take note of the players in this bi-weekly distraction.

GENE

What the heck are you talking about? You suck at poker, despite your keen observations. That is the difference between us.

CHUCK

Women are like cards.

KEITH

Women are like a lot of things.

CRAIG

Since the game is over and I've won as much as I can here, I'll bite. Why are women like cards?

CHUCK

Women come in 52 varieties, like the cards in this deck., but you constantly find yourself lacking the one needed to complete a winning hand.

GENE

Can you preach less and deal more?

CHUCK

I said that I was out.

CRAIG

I see money on the table.

CHUCK

You've won enough. Enjoy your empire.

CRAIG

I do ok. I play to win, and you are not children.

KEITH

They behave at times like children.

CHUCK

I'm taking it to the Willow. As far as people behaving Keith

KEITH

Taking what to the Willow?

CHUCK

My suave, debonair self.

KEITH

Your suave, debonair self? Has it finally arrive from Amazon? If you discover that it doesn't work at this Willow joint, remember that Amazon is very generous with returns. They even pay postage.

GENE

The Willow? Why didn't you say so? What about it Craig? Are you up for a repeat? You can buy us a drink with our lost wages if the ladies don't show.

KEITH

Which ladies are these?

GENE

She's hot.

CHUCK

Why is that a compliment? She will burn you. Kimberly Fredrichs has set more fires than last year's arsonist.

CRAIG

She is a woman whom one does not describe with monosyllabic adjectives. Hot diminishes her intensity. She is incandescent, enticing and taut.

CHUCK

Annacine must have taught you those fancy words.

KEITH

Where did you see her?

GENE

At the Willow, with Annacine.

KEITH

My Annacine?

CHUCK

She's yours if you can keep her.

GENE

Them's the breaks.

KEITH

What did you say?

CHUCK

About Annacine? Sorry. It was a joke.

KEITH

No, Gene. What you said about the brakes.

GENE

Them's the breaks. Sometimes the cards go your way and sometimes

CRAIG

Them ain't the breaks. It is pure skill on display.

GENE

Are we going to play cards or go to the Willow. I'm tired of talking and not following through.

CHUCK

They were kicking up their heels at the Willow. I've never seen anyone actually doing it.

KEITH

Doing what?

CHUCK

Kicking up their heels. You know, like this. Please try to follow the conversation, Keith. I figured that your wife must have selected it for their men, you know, characters. It didn't seem to be her type of place.

KEITH

What are you saying, Chuck?

GENE

You haven't been there?

KEITH

No, not yet.

GENE

It is not a meat market, but they serve a wonderful, smothered chicken? Get it?

KEITH

I'm beginning to. Where exactly is the new place located?

CHUCK

In Oldham County. As I was saying; with women, its either her hair or her shoes. Shoes are safer. Compliment her on her shoes. She doesn't expect it. Clever, don't you think?

GENE

Stupid is what I think. You must have read that in Cosmo.

CHUCK

It's also an indication if they are cheap, or halfway committed.

GENE

Committed to what?

CHUCK

If they have good shoes, they are serious in offering their best efforts. It's a tell, like in poker.

GENE

You wouldn't recognize a tell if he shot an arrow from your head. Some of your ideas, they might be valuable if we all lived in Ozland with you. Look at a woman's shoes! Are you one of those feet guys? I'm glad this table doesn't have a glass top. You pay attention to the unimportant facets of poker and women. I can't understand how you made it through medical school.

CHUCK

If you had done it yourself, you would be able to understand.

KEITH

What happened at the Willow?

CHUCK

Nothing.

KEITH

And yet you plan on returning?

GENE

If at first you don't succeed...

CHUCK

That is the same losing strategy that I employ in poker.

GENE

It absolutely is. Who says that I'm not observant? Oh yeah, you! But you have so much fun that I've decided to try it. With a beer chaser. Lucky at cards. I forget how it goes. Are you with us Craig? The night is young and so are we. And you hold our wallets.

KEITH

I told you they behave like children. Are you going to chaperone them?

CRAIG

Maybe next time boys. I have work to do in the morning.

CHUCK

It's been fun for you tonight, Craig. Stop by if you change your mind. (*Gene and Chuck exit*)

CRAIG

Those two would not recognize incandescence if their feet were aflame. They are more accustomed to rescuing electronic maidens in video games, than in conversing with a confident female.

KEITH

What did Chuck intend with that crack about your empire?

CRAIG

Jealousy.

KEITH

That's good.

CRAIG

'That's good' is an unexpected response.

KEITH

It's good to be envied.

CRAIG

That sounds like the contents of a fortune cookie. Chuck discovered that I have a few shops, more than the one you've seen.

KEITH

A few?

CRAIG

More than a few.

KEITH

Are you finding everything that you need in the garage?

CRAIG

I am. Many of the parts were intermingled, while others are poorly labeled. The old junk should be tossed.

KEITH

I plan on trashing it very soon.

CRAIG

Those imported parts should go as well. They are not worth the risk of breakdown or worse. Here is an example, see how easy it broke? (*rertrieves from end table, and hands to Keith ,a section of brake tubing in two pieces*)

KEITH

Thanks. That must be one of the Chinese knockoffs I bought before I realized that you get what you pay for. I'll ditch those.

CRAIG

Just as long as you do before they send you into a ditch. I can mark the ones with red tape if that would help. That way you can make the final decision to keep or toss.

KEITH

That would be a big help. By the way, is there anything else in the house you have your eye on?

CRAIG

You have that one delicious baby from 1950s. You wouldn't be hiding a well sprung racer in its own bedroom?

KEITH

What?

CRAIG

A turned 70s corvette. That, or something newer, but just as racy. I've only seen this room and the garage, but from the outside it's obvious that the house is a regular chateau. Its big, and I've learned that most rich people do rich things. They like to fill their houses with..

KEITH

I'm not rich.

CRAIG

You rub shoulders with the rich every day. Listen Keith, I don't mean to offend you.

KEITH

You haven't offended me. Tell me more; you still have a chance or two remaining.

CRAIG

The wealthy act wealthy by flaunting their eccentricity. Not all, but a lot of the rich do. Many of my clients...

KEITH

Is that why I'm doing?

CRAIG

So far, not at all. I find it curious. Your behavior is rare.

KEITH

Is that a compliment?

CRAIG

Purely an observation. Let me describe a typical client, say a man your age who owned a car like yours. It would not be their only classic ride. A rich guy acquires things in sets. A set of one is the best, like Codex Gates, but those are unique and unaffordable unless you are in the top handful of people on the planet. Instead, they compromise by picking up a couple of Picassos, a pair of special guns, or, and this is where I see it, a stable of cars. Regular rich people aren't content with one of anything. It keeps them

KEITH

Satisfied?

CRAIG

I was going to say entertained for a while. Acquisition is distraction. In my experience what rich man has only one car? Very few.

I theorized that you might act similarly, even though you're not rich, but maybe just maybe you might like to have another ride something younger that has more modern curves and that handles unusual maneuvers better, and that provide a more exhilarating ride.

KEITH

What are we talking about Craig?

CRAIG

The 50s babe is nice for touring but on a hot summer day on a winding road a more modern sports car can be sweet very hot, yeah maybe too hot for many of my clients. But you, well, you might have a 63 split window corvette squirreled away, in its climate-controlled garage disguised as a bedroom in the far wing, so maybe the wife doesn't know about it.

KEITH

This makes for an intriguing theory Craig, very intriguing but as I said I'm not rich. I'll stick with the DeSoto Mopar all the way. The split window I will leave to you to cherish.

CRAIG

You are a rare guy. I've enjoyed tonight, thanks for having invited me.

KEITH

Enjoy your spoils.

CRAIG

My spoils?

KEITH

Your winnings.

CRAIG

Oh, yeah. Goodnight. (*exits*)

KEITH

I don't mind getting my hands dirty. I agree to work up a sweat in a good cause.

In a few days, the curtain will rise, the DeSoto and the wife will exit fiery stage left, and I will be rid of both these women. And for a while, as long as the scene demands, Kimberly shall be kissed as she never has been before. Or since.

(*Turns the pieces of brake lining in his hand*)

And Craig, dear mechanical Craig. He will be left with this as a souvenir, a small reward for having kept Annacine distracted. Them's the breaks.

(*places brake lining away in drawer and wipes hand on a napkin from the poker table*)

I worried that my plan would implode before it had the opportunity to explode. I need them both, but separately. Speaking aloud on stage to oneself has until this exact moment struck me as being pretentious and ridiculous. Now, I understand. It is both pretentious and ridiculous, yet despite its shortcomings, I find it exceedingly useful. I require them both, until the curtain on Annacine's play has fallen. Who claims that we men aren't clever, but only lucky?

(*spots wine glass above drawer*)

What's this? A well placed prop that I can utilize in my own ad lib. Craig will be part of this after all, a small but respectable part. Greedy and hungry fit equally well a crossword puzzle clue.

ACT II

SCENE 4

(Detectives Emily Muse and Jason Silver await the arrival of Keith in his living room)

JASON

She has been gone for nearly five minutes. Where could she have gone?

EMILY

This is a very big house, and this is the only room we've seen.

JASON

Do you think that she has a clue?

EMILY

Our role is to investigate crime, not to spoil a marriage by speaking too soon.

JASON

She is a mystery writer. Naturally, she must have an inkling that her husband is up to something. In my experience, women reside permanently in suspect mode.

EMILY

It's safer, if sadder. Which is why we make for superior detectives.

JASON

Men transform our suspicions into effective action.

EMILY

Did you read that on Reddit?

JASON

Which is why we make for superior detectives.

EMILY

There isn't much to see in this room that we haven't seen already. While we wait, let's recap your theory.

You suspect that Annacine Finley suspects Keith Finley.

So what? Asking her won't help anyone.

Is our role to suspect him and his suspected girlfriend Kimberly Fredrichs are...and what about that new guy? Just so you can speak to the wife in private?

This is too many suspects for any detective, man or woman, to play with.

JASON

But for a pair of detectives?

EMILY

But we already have our suspicions. These are well founded suspicions based on written evidence. Isn't that why we were hired as detectives to begin with? If you question her, you may let slip a word or a phrase and it will all be canceled, as if nothing was ever planned. It will be roses instead of carnations. In your mind, we have three suspects, and we haven't left the one room in this house. I sincerely hope that we aren't offered a tour of the house. If so, I will let you question the thirty or so more suspects that we trip over. In addition, there is no crime. One crime is my minimum. It should be for you as well. Unless we have both misread the job posting, specifically the part about us being investigating detectives, and not writers of mystery yarns.

JASON

I should have asked her when I had the chance. She may not return.

EMILY

You will have to wait. We are two detectives here on official police business to talk with Keith Finley about the upcoming charity bike ride. This is not for fun and games.

JASON

It is obvious that you have never been on a charity bike ride. I should speak to Annacine.

EMILY

It is too soon. After

JASON

After may be too late.

EMILY

After the 'bike ride' will be soon enough. This is an important case for both of us.

JASON

There is no crime. So that means that I can broach the subject to...

EMILY

This is official police business with her husband. Anything else is out of scope. The fact that Keith Finley sits on the Police-Citizen board provides a good cover for this visit.

JASON

What if I mention the Doctor Evy murder? That would be an in, and then later she and I could speak about the other topic. Preventing and solving murders is official police and besides its good community relations.

Annacine Finley is an upstanding member of the community and would be glad to assist us.

EMILY

The Evy murder?

JASON

A married couple, and the husband, Doctor Evy, is found dead, under, quote, mysterious circumstances.

EMILY

I remember.

JASON

It happened only a week ago.

EMILY

And he was either murdered, or suicided, or killed in self-defense.

JASON

Yes, him.

EMILY

Or all three, but that would prove extremely difficult for one person to accomplish, even for a doctor.

JASON

So is his wife, you know. A doctor. Doctor Evy, the husband that is, was an upstanding citizen, the same as Annacine Finley

EMILY

He will never stand up again.

JASON

Point taken.

EMILY

What is it that you are failing to tell me, Jason?

JASON

I wonder if the Finleys knew him? If so, I could speak at length with Annacine.

EMILY

To your credit you are persistent. Remember; it is not our case.

JASON

Does that make it not our job? Detective Percheron should know about the connection.

EMILY

Which connection? Do you want to call him and tell him how to do his job?

JASON

I didn't say that. Besides, it is not our case. Still, it interests me. I've decided to pretend to work on it.

EMILY

You are going to pretend to work on an imaginary case, because someone you met a minute ago, may have known someone who may or may not have been murdered?

JASON

A bit tenuous, I agree. I'm thinking that if it was murder, that money was the motive. There was a prenup and the wife would not receive alimony. One can consider alimony as ransom. They sell ransom insurance, why not alimony insurance?

EMILY

You're a detective more or less. Figure it out.

JASON

I'm trying. I don't have it all worked out yet, but I have spare time to work on it.

EMILY

Don't you have a full-time job with the police? You really should take up writing fiction. Annacine Finley may in fact be willing to offer you a few tips. You don't seem to take this job seriously enough.

JASON

Look at the cases we have. This imaginary one with Keith Finley.

EMILY

You crave that sort of challenge.

JASON

Along with babysitting you.

EMILY

What did you just say?

JASON

When you were assigned to me, I was told

EMILY

Wait! You were assigned to me. And I was told that you needed special handling.

JASON

Ha!

EMILY

Unfortunately for me, they underestimated the level of care required.

JASON

You have it backwards. I was instructed to keep you out of trouble.

EMILY

That is true in your fantasy version. But...

JASON

We can settle this later.

EMILY

We can settle right now the fact that we are not working Detective Percheron's case, not least because he is my uncle. As far as I am concerned his case is as fictional as the ones in these mysteries.

JASON

You are so funny. Do you want us to solve a fictional case?

EMILY

It would be our second adventure.

JASON

Tell that to your uncle. I will stand right behind you.

EMILY

Leaving me to absorb the blast. How gallant. Jason, we are not paid to solve fiction. But go ahead, I have no doubt that the department's most successful homicide detective would relish his niece's new partner's input and the opinion of a mystery writer.

JASON

You are such a supportive person.

EMILY

If we fly anywhere together, I wonder if you could fly along for free as a service animal. You would look cute in a Wildcat's collar.

JASON

I'm a Cardinald fan. Emily, I am flabbergasted that your uncle,

EMILY

Everyone calls him Perch.

JASON

That Uncle Perch

EMILY

He is my uncle, not yours.

JASON

That Mister P has not pulled rank and joined us here tonight.

EMILY

Should I text dear uncle?

(*Jason steps to bookshelf and selects a book, just as Annacine, Keith, and Kimberly enter*)

JASON

May I?

ANNACINE

Of course. Be my guest.

JASON

Check the brakes.

ANNACINE

That was my first book. It didn't sell as well as the subsequent ones. But well enough to encourage me to continue.

KEITH

You are being modest dear

KIMBERLY

That is so unlike you.

JASON

I've read this one, recently. Its

KIMBERLY

It's what?

JASON

It's interesting.

ANNACINE

Thanks. Interesting is such a deflating compliment. Does that mean that you caught the killer on page three?

JASON

No. Actually

EMILY

Don't say another word, Jason. That is, I want to read it myself and you're going to ruin it for me.

KIMBERLY

Never give the ending away in this house.

JASON

I apologize, Mrs.

ANNACINE

Annacine, please. Are you a couple? I've been told that I can be blunt.

EMILY

We are partners.

JASON

Annacine. Sometimes I get carried away.

ANNACINE

Young people have so many arrangements. We used the phrase being coy. These days, words mean less and less. They are in the process of losing all meaning. Someday soon, we will revert to grunting. Where will that leave my writing? The good news is that I won't have to spell check anything and I can dispense with a proofreader.

EMILY

I'm sorry that I was not clear. I did not seek to confuse you. We are partners, police detectives. We stopped by to confirm with Mr. Finely that all is set for the upcoming bike ride next month. I suppose that I could have called or texted but,

JASON

It's my fault. I pressured Emily to drive us here.

ANNACINE

Emily doesn't strike me as a person who succumbs to pressure.

EMILY

He asked politely.

KIMBERLY

He whined? Women pout, men whine.

ANNACINE

You two aren't an item?

JASON

Just friends, or partners. We work with Detective Percheron.

EMILY

That is not entirely correct. Jason and I are both failing to be clear tonight.

JASON

Not extremely closely, not every day.

ANNACINE

Perch? I know him very well. Keith, if I'm murdered make sure that he is assigned my case. These two can certainly assist.

EMILY

He is retiring in three weeks.

ANNACINE

That is a pity.

KEITH

I would not say that. Why is retirement a pity?

ANNACINE

Oh why isn't it? He is so talented.

KEITH

Everyone enjoys retirement.

ANNACINE

Detective Percheron is likely an exception.

KIMBERLY

Someone will need to give you a nudge (*jostles Annacine*) before the big day.

Keith shocked

ANNACINE

Which big day would that be?

KIMBERLY

This detective's retirement. He's apparently better at solving murders than you are at writing them.

KEITH

I would not go that far, Kimberly.

ANNACINE

Nor would I. I must solve them first to write them

KIMBERLY

If you want to see which of you is the champion, you will need to die soon.

KEITH

Kimberly!

KIMBERLY

You can't very well solve your own murder. Can you?

ANNACINE

That's an idea too late now.

KEITH

I'm sorry that you two detectives had to drive all this way this evening. I expect that you want to verify that all is well regarding the charity bike ride. If you have any further questions later, please call or text.

EMILY

Just as I told you Jason. Thanks for seeing us and sorry for the disturbance. I believe that we have concluded our business, Detective Silver.

JASON

We have? Yes, we have.

EMILY

Thank you for confirming the status of the bike ride, Mr. Finley.

KEITH

Please, call me Keith. Thanks for stopping by. It was nice to see you two again.

ANNACINE

You may take the book, if you like.

JASON

Absolutely.

ANNACINE

Let me sign it for you.

JASON

It's Detective Silver.

ANNACINE

Oh, that won't do. I've asked you to call me Annacine. Surely, I can inscribe something more intimate than Detective Silver.

JASON

Jason.

ANNACINE

To dearest Jason, XOXO, Annacine. That's better.

EMILY

Perfect. We need to leave now, before my partner faints.

ACT II

SCENE 5

(A few minutes later, Kimberly and Keith)

KIMBERLY

Did you notice how she had the male detective call her Annacine?

KEITH

Was she flirting? (*Laughs*) Annacine flirting? Ha. But lately.

KIMBERLY

Lately what?

KEITH

She is different, is that it? You've noticed it too, haven't you.

KIMBERLY

It's simply a phase. Consider it as you would a new hairstyle.

KEITH

Annacine doesn't get new hairstyles. Everything is a phase until it phases into something else. I'm glad we are going ahead

KIMBERLY

Are you?

KEITH

Ten days. What did you mean a moment ago?

KIMBERLY

What did I say? You know me, I forget my lines.

KEITH

You asked me if I noticed that Annacine told the male detective to use her given name.

KIMBERLY

Was she flirting?

KEITH

You just said that she wasn't flirting.

KIMBERLY

Oh yes. I remember now. It irritated me. She was the only Mrs. in the room, and she knew it.

KEITH

But the detective didn't know that she was the only Mrs.

KIMBERLY

That is my point. He could have been speaking to me. I was the last one to speak to him.

KEITH

He didn't? But I thought..

KIMBERLY

What he knows or knew is not important. Annacine didn't know what he knew, so he could have just as easily have been speaking to me and not her.

KEITH

You are beginning to lose me.

KIMBERLY

That had better not be true.

KEITH

Is there a point to this know and knew?

KIMBERLY

Annacine acted as if I wasn't there.

KEITH

It is her house.

KIMBERLY

That is no excuse for her behavior.

KEITH

I see.

KIMBERLY

You do? Good.

KEITH

And you think that her mistreatment of you

KIMBERLY

I would not describe it as mistreatment

KEITH

Will extend to me. She's changing. I don't like this phase stuff at all. The old Annacine would never flirt or think of quitting me. Ten days and we will put an end to this new Annacine.

KIMBERLY

Tonight's near fiasco could have all been avoided. Why did you invite those two detectives over this evening? Are you insane?

KEITH

How would I know? This scheme is so unlike me.

KIMBERLY

That's wrong. This is so very much who you are, who we are. It's the type of people we are. I'm not ashamed of my nature.

KEITH

Kimberly, what began as a simple idea germinated by wine, has now blossomed into this big complex production.

KIMBERLY

The wife will be dead and buried in ten days.

KEITH

Ten days.

KIMBERLY

You must hold on and act normally until then. It's less than two weeks.

KEITH

It sounds like a long time.

KIMBERLY

Why did you invite those homicide detectives to the house, tonight of all nights? If you were my husband, I would slap you.

KEITH

I am not your husband.

KIMBERLY

No, you aren't. (*Kimberly punches Keith in the shoulder*).

KEITH

You are one to talk, with your comment about giving Annacine a nudge. For your information, I often invite police to the house to discuss the law enforcement community bicycle race that we hold as a charity event. It is that time of year, in less than a month.

KIMBERLY

That's twice as long as ten days.

KEITH

Ten days.

KIMBERLY

But why them?

KEITH

It was just a coincidence. They are on the bike ride committee. And for your information, I did not invite them. That crazy Jason has fan fever for Annacine. His partner said as much.

KIMBERLY

This is even worse. We have a puppy love puppy yipping around where he should not be. I thought detectives were clever, but not ridiculous. You are planning to murder your wife and you dismiss a coincidence involving those two.

(*Kimberly punches Keith again*)

KEITH

Stop that. If you want a boxing partner, drive over to Milestone.

KIMBERLY

You know what type of partner I need. (*pause*)

How long after the big event will the two of us endure?

KEITH

Who knows? We both understood this to be a means to an end.

KIMBERLY

A means to an end in more ways than one.

KEITH

The buzz will fade, and we will go our separate ways.

KIMBERLY

And if the buzz does not fade?

KEITH

We play our roles until it does. Kimberly, we must be honest.

KIMBERLY

Honest? Honestly?

KEITH

I will settle for serious. Romance is serious business. It is purely a question of when and not if. I will play my role of dutiful husband, you will manage your affairs, your business affairs, clothes, things like that. Don't pout, I've allotted you a princely allowance, a decent cut of the profits.

KIMBERLY

Clothes are important, Keith.

KEITH

I've already agreed to everything you requested to be part of this, oh where was I?

KIMBERLY

Over there, pontificating.

KEITH

If the buzz does not fade, you and I will continue to act the same, the detectives will play their roles.

KIMBERLY

Will they? For how long? There are so many demands on their time, they may drop it.

KEITH

So much the better.

KIMBERLY

Do you believe it would be better? Replacements may prove less effective, but they can ruin everything we've built.

KEITH

After me, your next boyfriend will fall asleep after the aperitif.

KIMBERLY

I love that word. Only the French could marry foreplay with alcohol.

KEITH

Come here, sit beside me. Let's rehearse together one more time. I've decided to donate something to the police benevolence society. That is my parting gift, as I'm leaving that board, among others.

It will be a corkscrew, a twisting road, an abrupt, pointy end, and then a whiff of new life.

KIMBERLY

Let's leave here and rehearse in the regular spot.

(*Kimberly and Keith exit*)

(*Doorbell, Annacine answers and Rachel enters*)

ANNACINE

I should hire a butler to answer the door. Or an electrician to dewire the doorbell. I thought we celebrities practiced don't call me, I'll call you.

RACHEL

You would find it more electrifying if you hired a private investigator. The things I do for you without recompense.

ANNACINE

What is it now? Let me rephrase the question. Who is it now? Kimberly?

RACHEL

Kimberly Fredrichs? I did think that it was her.

ANNACINE

It? What is it? Was was it that it was her.

RACHEL

It is it. You know. It. It. It may still be her, Kimberly Fredrichs that is, but I have information from another source, one devious but trustworthy that I am still checking.

ANNACINE

Devious but trustworthy? They must have a pair of those at the zoo.

RACHEL

It may be a ruse, or a double bluff, or an attempt at a payoff. I'm not sure. I need to be thorough before I make any accusations. Investigation is harder than you realize, Annacine. And I'm doing this work pro bono. That means for free.

ANNACINE

Where do you find the time, Rachel? You dream up plots more quickly that I can. If not Kimberly, then who plays the mysterious woman?

RACHEL

You must have spoken to her. She left your house not more than five minutes ago.

ANNACINE

That would be Kimberly.

RACHEL

(*pulls out and consults notebook and her watch*) I saw her leave with Keith. Kimberly must be his cover for the other woman. The other subject left ten minutes ago. Sorry, but time flies when you are on an active stakeout. Any questions?

ANNACINE

My questions serve merely to delay you and confuse me. Please continue your....report.

RACHEL

She was young, and she left with an equally young man. I've seen the two of them together before, and I've seen her with Keith.

ANNACINE

You must mean the police detectives. I wonder if they detected your surveillance. They had business with Keith, something about a charity bike ride. The female detective is named Emily Muse.

RACHEL

I never trust women named Emily. With a name like Emily, the parents were up to something.

ANNACINE

I have no doubt that they were up to something.

RACHEL

Emily is too innocent to be genuine. She must be his alibi.

ANNACINE

Emily is Keith's alibi for Kimberly, and Kimberly is Keith's alibi for Emily. I cannot imagine a man selecting two worse alibis or two more suspicious women than Kimberly and Emily. Emily is a police detective for heaven's sake. This is all perfectly innocent.

RACHEL

Never trust innocence.

ANNACINE

Never trust innocence. What a perfect title for a murder mystery. I wonder if it works for a romance.

RACHEL

Abandon romance. Delay your departure. I have never appeared in your stories. Nor did my husband. Why is that?

ANNACINE

You are a friend. To murder you would be an insult, akin to throwing you a bone. Not a bone, not for a friend.

RACHEL

But a complete skeleton would have been appreciated. See, I can model; dead, dying, prostrate. This room can be your stage. Have you a knife?

ANNACINE

Not handy.

RACHEL

And my poor departed Stevie. He would have made an excellent corpse before he died. Now he is dead, his chance lost. Forget romance. Your hands are strong enough for one more pushing, a pleasant stabbing with a sharp, pointed blade. Maybe Keith as victim. There is something out of kilter. Are you willfully blind?

ANNACINE

Why do you say Keith? If I were destitute and constantly inebriated, you would blame Keith.

RACHEL

If you won't slay friends and you have not stumbled across a suitable stranger, then who remains?

ANNACINE

Not Keith.

RACHEL

Then it falls to me to be your final victim.

ANNACINE

Why this obsession with being in a book?

RACHEL

I want to be noticed for something. I notice but remain myself unnoticed. Is it too much to ask? Keith notices.

ANNACINE

Please, not Keith again.

RACHEL

And then there is you and Craig.

ANNACINE

There is no me and Craig. Why is everyone close to me including me in their works of imagination? I don't enjoy being a character in your romance and intrigue. It's bad fiction.

RACHEL

It's not fiction. I have it all jotted down here. This is true life, Annacine.

ANNACINE

Life is fiction. Good night, Rachel. (*exits*)

RACHEL

If Annacine won't have it out with her husband, I shall. Wives know most about their husband and the little they don't, they choose not to.

What are friends for, if not to meddle at the appropriate hour? Keith is a sly one, but he is only a man. He has eluded and confused me, but he has thrown me for the final time.

ACT II

SCENE 6

(A theatre stage with the curtain down, a set which to all intents and purposes is the living room of Annacine and Keith. A few photos are different, a chair a different color, the potted plant in its place)

KEITH

My wife was angry, and she took the car. It was still being repaired, and either she forgot or did not care. The Desoto was a reminder of the early days of our marriage, and it accompanied us on a romantic trip that has lasted until...

The car was older than either of us, and when we rode in it together, we could be and feel young again.

I should have sold it, but it seemed so reliable.

JASON

It was a shame about the DeSoto. What was she angry about?

KEITH

I will never know. You know how women get sometimes.

When we were just married, and my wife was so set on publishing a novel, the car represented a tradeoff, a wager you might say.

JASON

She used that once in a book. Is that correct?

KEITH

Yes, her first mystery. It was a tradeoff between the book and her career. If her first book did not do well, then I'd have sold the DeSoto. The car appeared on the book's cover. Was it Karma, do you suppose?

JASON

Is that the model of the DeSoto?

KEITH

No. It was a DeSoto Firedome.

EMILY

It was as you suggested. The brake lines were substandard and had not been tested by the installer. It was a matter of poor timing. If your wife had waited until the work had been completed and checked, we wouldn't be here today. We spoke to the mechanic, and he is as sorry as we are.

KEITH

If she had only waited.

EMILY

Yes, if only she had waited.

KEITH

I see. Still, that might be called Karma. Was it divine justice or turnabout is unfair play? I cannot say, except that I need rationalization in that her life was complete, if brief. Her life ended almost as life imitating art imitating life. Art and life, I suppose that I will not be able to appreciate either in quite the same way again. The gods raise up whom they wish to destroy.

EMILY

Again, we are sorry for your loss sir. It was such a needless accident. No one could have survived a drop from such a height. It was a shame that the car had no seat belts.

KEITH

We wanted to keep the car as original as possible. We thought, I believed, foolishly I see clearly now, that somehow the DeSoto and the two of us would never change, never needed improvement. That was a mistake. Hubris is the word, I think.

Thank you again for your efforts and resolution on this unfortunate accident, detectives. My thanks especially to you, Lieutenant Goldman.

JASON

You are welcome, sir. We will leave you now. Again, our condolences.

(*Detectives leave and Kimberly enters a moment later*)

KIMBERLY

It's strange, you rehearse, and you rehearse, but it is not real until you act. The pretense is the reality at that moment.

KEITH

It's over now.

KIMBERLY

The hard part is over. Our run is just beginning darling.

ACT II

SCENE 7

KIMBERLY

Why are you still here, in this mirage of a home?

KEITH

I want to enjoy this moment as long as possible. It may be over tomorrow; they may knock on the door in morning, and this wonderful moment will be just a memory.

KIMBERLY

Keith, we can't stay here forever.

KEITH

Can't we? I'm perfectly happy here. This is perfect, exactly as I imagined it. Remember all of the planning and rehearsals? And then events just whirled by according to script. Can you believe that we did it?

KIMBERLY

It was all you Keith I had very little to do with it

KEITH

Don't be modest Kimberly, you contributed so much. Did you see the look on Jason's face during his 'interrogation' of me? He must have truly believed I was going to confess despite all of rehearsals you and I went through. And Emily, she looked lost toward the end. I have to give her credit; she nearly caught us. I wonder what her uncle, the great Percheron, would have done?

KIMBERLY

It does not matter. He was not involved. We pulled it off.

KEITH

A toast to the erstwhile detectives.

KIMBERLY

I wish this were good wine and did not have the taste of colored water.

KEITH

We will share an excellent bottle from Annacine's cellar.

KIMBERLY

It's time to go.

KEITH

So soon? This has been exhausting. I really could sleep for weeks. So much preparation and detailed planning, the near catastrophe with Annacine's friend Rachel.

KIMBERLY

I'm ready for bed as well, but not one shared with a snorer.

KEITH

Who claims that I snore?

KIMBERLY

Your wife, your sister.

KEITH

I have no sister.

KIMBERLY

If a sister were incarnated here, she would swear that you roar. Women know the truth: all men snore; it is only a question of decibel level. My guess is that you won't sleep tonight. Nor will they.

KEITH

Why is that?

KIMBERLY

A woman's intuition.

KEITH

Women's intuition explains everything and nothing. The deed is done as they say. No use crying over spilled wine, genuine or false. Who is the they you mentioned.

KIMBERLY

Are you blind? Can you not see that the detectives are an item in the making. They acted their roles as best they could, but I'm certain they had other pursuits more pressing than chasing you. They are as much amateurs as we are. Besides, they have their own romance which will outlast ours. You've been completely focused on your own passion to the point of oblivion. Now that it's over perhaps you can turn you attention to the woman who merits it.

KEITH

You have been incredibly supportive.

KIMBERLY

The words all women yearn to hear. That role becomes wearisome

KEITH

I ask for a bit more time.

KIMBERLY

As agreed. No more than that Keith. We pulled it off. It was incredibly easy, easier than either of us thought. You were marvelous darling. (*Exaggerated, deep voice*)

She did not suspect anything until the last moment. And when the final curtain came down, she must have been as surprised as anyone ever has been.

(*Emily and Jason enter*)

EMILY

My uncle, Detective Percheron sends his congratulations.

KEITH

He does?

EMILY

He rarely praises a murderer but, in your case, you made an exception. You can imagine that he has investigated some strange cases, some involving celebrities, but yours was among the most satisfying, despite that he was not even backstage so to speak, but purely a distant observer.

KEITH

How did he know?

EMILY

Does it matter?

KEITH

I suppose not.

EMILY

You too Kimberly. Uncle Perch sends his regards.

KIMBERLY

That's very generous but really this was all Keith's work.

KEITH

You're much too modest Kimberly. It was both of us.

JASON

He's waiting for us downtown. We are having a sort of party you might say.

KEITH

A party?

EMILY

Jason exaggerates. He is a budding novelist, like your wife once was.

JASON

The senior detective is hosting an informal get together. We need to leave now, I'm afraid. Of course, Keith, you must bring your

(*Annacine enters. Keith and Kimberly show fear, because they can't anticipate her reaction*)

ANNACINE

How could you do such a thing, Keith? And you Kimberly, conspiring behind my back?

KEITH/KIMBERLY

We thought...

(*Craig and Rachel enter*)

ANNACINE

You thought that I would enjoy being murdered?

CRAIG

I certainly did.

ANNACINE

You did?

CRAIG

Sure. The ending was a clever twist. It was a fantastic show that leaves the audience wanting more. A sequel, you know. Don't you do the same?

ANNACINE

I haven't until now. Perhaps I will. Romance repeats. I only have one word for you two, Bravo. These past weeks have been so confusing and distressing."

KEITH

Sorry, hon. Them's the breaks, so to speak.

ANNACINE

I did not know what to think. I felt a character in one of my own books. No, in the book of another author, where I was not in control of my own self, by own decisions. But it was worth it. Bravo.

KEITH

We had to make a few tweaks. By far the biggiest change was that in the original book, the wife did not die. Annacine wanted her kill the wife, you do have a bloodthirsty streak my dear, but I discouraged my wife from murdering a female lead. The book was successful, so successful, that it became a sort of taboo. Annacine, I was wrong, you were right.

EMILY

Pay attention Jason.

KEITH

And so tonight, I corrected my mistake from so many years ago.

EMILY

Are you two ready to go downtown? No handcuffs, but we can run the siren if you like. Uncle Perch's gift.

ANNACINE

That is very tempting, and thank Perch for the offer, but Keith and I have another offer at home.

JASON

Thanks for everything Keith. I suppose that soon we will be back to chasing real, less pleasant killers.

KEITH

Rachel, I'm sorry to have kept you in the dark for so long.

RACHEL

About what?

KEITH

Never mind.

RACHEL

About your recent secret meetings, your assignations. I have them all documented in here. Each and every one.

KEITH

They were rehearsals.

RACHEL

I still have my suspicions about you, Keith Finley. This entire production, the actors, the scripts, this set, it all strikes me as the actions of one clever man constructing a plausible cover story. It smells to me like a red herring.

ANNACINE

And to me like a wonderful anniversary gift.

EMILY

Now is the time, Jason. Ask Annacine your question

JASON

Annacine, I'd like to become a writer of mysteries. Will you help me?

EMILY

That was why we stopped at your house the other day, to check on the bike ride, and Jason planned to request your support. I convinced him to delay until after this play opened, until now.

ANNACINE

I will be delighted to help in any way that I can. Emily's uncle Perch and I have grown too old for murder, the younger generation deserves its moment in the morgue. I hope that he finds romance. As for myself I intend to dedicate myself to romance. Isn't that correct, Keith?

KEITH

Yes dear (*dead pan, then kisses her extravagantly*). Yes dear

EMILY

Annacine, since you and Keith can't accompany us tonight, perhaps Rachel would like to go to party in your stead? What do you think, Rachel?

RACHEL

Me?

EMILY

Uncle Perch gets everything right while, you, well not so much.

ANNACINE

Yes, opposites attract. I definitely agree that they should meet.

RACHEL

I'll go. I could use a second opinion on my investigation to date. But I'll be back on duty tomorrow morning Keith, so no more funny business.

(*Emily, Jason, and Rachel exit*)

CRAIG

That was quite the performance you too, but I confess Keith that I was jealous each time you kissed Kimberly.

KIMBERLY

You were? You must tell me all about it. I'm open to revision.

CRAIG

The DeSoto will be finished tomorrow.

ANNACINE

Check the brakes one more time.

KIMBERLY

Don't worry. I will do that with him. You can pick up the car in a few days.

(*Kimberly and Craig exit*)

KEITH

You heard her dear, we have a few days to kill. So to speak. Any ideas?

ANNACINE

Maybe.

KEITH

I saw that you wore new shoes tonight. They've fashionable and very becoming. They are perfect with your outfit.

ANNACINE

With all this, you notice my shoes?

KEITH

I notice all of you. Annacine, you are the world itself.

ANNACINE

That is a good start.

KEITH

Any ideas honey?

ANNACINE

Something romantic. Let's decide together.

FIN

THEM AIN'T THE BREAKS by Gregory John Ferris

www.ingramcontent.com/pod-product-compliance
Lightning Source LLC
Chambersburg PA
CBHW030343310726
48979CB00001B/163
9798218107239